IN HIS OWN DEFENSE

ISBN-13:   978-1481089012

ISBN-10:   1481089013

ACKNOWLEDGMENTS

This book would not have been possible without the support of my family and friends, including my virtual friends at opensalon.com and oursalon.com and my amazing Facebook network of readers. I thank you for continuing to read my blog posts, for allowing me to pursue my dream of writing, and hope that you will find this effort worthy of your time.

I also want to specifically extend my gratitude to the following people:

To Diana Ani Stokely, for her fantastic cover artwork.

To my parents: the man whom I strive to emulate (at least his positive traits) and the woman who has served, proudly, as my biggest fan for the past 47 years; as well as to my sister, Carin, for her support and tireless efforts at promoting my writings over the past several years.

To my daughters, Sara, Dani, and Alina, for their love and support, and to my four-legged son, DJ. They have inspired some of my favorite work, and hopefully they will be as proud of me as I am of them.

Most importantly, it is impossible for me to properly express my gratitude to my day-time wife, Karen, for her invaluable help over these past nine years and for her assistance with the Portuguese translations in this book, or to my full-time wife, Jennifer, for her continued (and, to some, inexplicable) love and support over the past quarter-century, and especially for her understanding when I was writing this book and/or my blogs and therefore not acting as a husband or father. I love you both (in different ways, of course).

CHAPTER I

"It is the duty of a lawyer to preserve his client's confidences. This duty outlasts the lawyer's employment, and extends as well to his employees."

- American Bar Association Canons of Professional Ethics Paragraph 37

"Tell me the truth, do I really need an attorney to do this, or can I do it myself?" asked the man in the brown leather chair. He leaned forward, yellow legal pad perched on his knee, and twisted a pen between the thumb and forefinger of his right hand. His glasses fell slightly to the tip of his nose, and he waited for an answer from the man seated behind the desk.

Eric Goldberg took a deep breath and, trying to collect his thoughts, looked intently at the fidgeting man. The conversation between the two men had been ongoing for over forty minutes now, most of which were taken up by the man, whose name Eric could not even remember, talking about how much he wanted to get a divorce from his cheating wife. This question, however, was never a good signal. It was the first question usually raised by the person who was merely looking for advice as to how he could act as his own lawyer, and signaled to Eric that he had now wasted the last forty minutes of his life.

He looked at the wall behind the man, focusing on the diplomas which bore his name and which now looked yellowed with time. The diplomas reminded him of a time long ago, when he first graduated from law school and looked forward to a fulfilling and exciting career in the law. Those hopes, however, had long ago been dashed, and he was now relegated to meeting with moochers who wanted to take his knowledge and advice without any real thought of compensating him for his time. "Well," he began after a deep sigh, "I can't say for sure that you need an attorney for your divorce, but…"

"I mean, it should be a simple case, right?" the man interrupted. "She will keep the kids. You told me that child support is set by the court, and we do not have anything like a house to worry about. So why would I need an attorney?"

The clock on Eric's desk read 6:24 p.m. Eric looked down at his shirt, wrinkled from his eleven-hour work day, and at the striped tie which fell slightly to the left of his slightly-too-large stomach. A half-full cup of cold coffee stood next to the clock, where it had been sitting since noon. Eric reached for the cup, took a deep gulp of the cold coffee, and replied, slowly and deliberately, "my belief is that you should always have legal representation for things of a legal nature, like divorces, because attorneys know the laws, they know the procedures, and they know the judges."

He looked at the man, who was furiously scribbling notes on his legal pad. "If a person tries to handle things themselves and messes up on the procedure, it could prove to be a problem in the actual divorce, or, more importantly, thereafter, especially when money and children are involved. You must remember, the divorce does not completely end your relationship with your wife, and you have to make sure that all of the future possibilities are taken care of now." He placed the coffee cup back on his desk, slightly to the left of the sticky ring left by coffee cups past.

The man stopped writing. He thumbed through his notes, and looked at some papers that he had put into a folder in anticipation of that evening's meeting. After a brief pause, he pulled out the printout of the internet page where he had found Eric's address and phone number. Staring at that page, he asked "So, if I were to retain your services for my divorce, what exactly is it that you would do for me again?"

"Seriously?" Eric thought, as he strained his eyes to see exactly what the man was reading. What had they been discussing since 5:40 that afternoon? This was one of the worst parts of his job, he lamented. The late meetings were not a problem when they led to money. The late meetings that were a waste of his time were a different story. Not that he had to run home, mind you. The apartment was quiet. Since his divorce had been finalized, things were much different. He used to get home, usually late, and see his wife and son, Jason. Now, his commute was only five minutes from the office, and the only activity in his apartment was his dog and Jason, when he decided to come home instead of staying out until all hours with his friends from the community college. His wife still lived in his old house, the house that he could no longer enter and which he only saw on occasion, when retrieving old files that were still stored in its attic.

He glanced down at the calendar on his desk, searching quickly for the man's name. "Let's start again from the beginning, Steve," he said slowly, "the first step is filing the complaint for divorce. We prepare the complaint based on the information that you give to me. Then we sign it and send it to the court to be filed. Once we have it back from the court, we then serve the complaint on your wife." He paused, noting that Steve had again begun to scribble furiously on his note pad.

After a few seconds, Steve, without looking up from his note pad and in mid-scribble, asked, "and what exactly does the Complaint say?"

"There are several parts to the Complaint, including various certifications that you will have to sign. I will need for you to give me a bunch of information about yourself, your wife, kids, date of marriage, stuff like that. Then I take all of the information, put it into the proper format, and have you come back to sign the complaint so we can file it with the court."

"The proper format," Steve replied, "what exactly is the proper format?" The tip of his pen sat on the legal pad, his right hand quivering slightly as he prepared to write. Now Eric knew for sure. There was no way that Steve Sanderson was retaining him to represent him in his divorce matter. Steve Sanderson's goal now was to get as much information as he could from Eric, then prepare the papers himself. Eric had been down this road before. And he was determined not to let it happen again.

"The proper format is the format that the court needs in order to comply with the statute and allow you to get divorced." Eric replied as he looked to the right, out the window of his office. It was starting to get dark outside, unexpected on this mid-June day, and Eric suspected that the rains that had been predicted on the news that morning were about to erupt. "I will show you after we prepare the Complaint."

"Do you have someone else's that you can show me now?" Steve asked, "or a template that you use so that I know what information you need? That way I can tell you exactly what you will need, and can also get you whatever papers you want as soon as possible." He put his pen down on the edge of Eric's desk and extended his right hand, as if to receive the gift of papers to review.

Eric, however, did not lean forward to the man to hand him any papers. In fact, he recoiled slightly, again scanning the diplomas hanging behind the man's head and outstretched arm. The Rutgers University diploma loomed behind and to the left of the man's head, bearing the year 1993. To its right, its bottom half obscured, was the diploma from Seton Hall University Law

School, a regal-looking paper which contained the year 1996. The diplomas, and the promise that they once represented, now mocked him. Perhaps appropriately for his mood, he could hear the ominous rumble of thunder outside as the skies grew ever darker, as the sound of the thunder obscured the traffic noise from Broad Street below.

"No, I don't," Eric replied, as the clock changed to 6:29. He shifted forward in his chair, the creaking of its movement joining with the sound of the door opening and closing in the outside office. Eric could now hear the rain striking the window to his right. He looked at the window, which bore the marks of pelting raindrops, making Eric wonder when the rain had begun and why he had not even noticed it until now. "I don't have a copy to show you, and I am not going to tell you the exact format so that you can do it yourself," he said softly, almost inaudibly. He straightened his back and said, in a more appropriate tone and volume of voice, "and I don't mean to be rude, but I think that my next client just walked in. Are you going to retain me to represent you or not?"

The man in the leather chair seemed surprised by the question. "I'm sorry," he gasped, "but I don't think that I like your attitude." He placed the cap back on his pen and reached down for the folder at his feet. "That question is pressuring me, and I don't think that is right. I was going to ask you to be my lawyer, but now

I don't think that I will," he said, taking the pad off of his knee and shoving it into the folder. "That's not very professional."

Eric stared into the man's eyes. "With all due respect, sir," he answered, "you and I both know that you weren't intending to work with me beyond this meeting. You came here looking for information. I never saw you reach for a checkbook. You never offered to sign an agreement." His voice growing louder, he snarled, "so don't lie to me and tell me that my attitude is bad. I deserve better. You want a professional? Show some respect."

The man was speechless, and a little nervous at what Eric might do next based on his tone of voice. He rose from his seat, hesitantly, folder tucked under his right armpit, and turned toward the door. "Good luck with the divorce," Eric said as the man walked out the door, silently, "don't screw it up." He knew that the last comment was, in fact, unprofessional and improper. At this point, however, he was fuming not only at the man, but the situation. It was after 6:30. Most people were already done with their work day. He had been at his desk since 7:30 that morning dealing with other people's problems. This guy complained that his wife was cheating on him. Eric thought of his own ex-wife. Perhaps this was the reason that she had cheated on him, because of all of the late nights at the office.

They had never really discussed the reasons for her infidelity, but he assumed that it was the many nights that she was forced to spend alone. The nights when he would not return to the house until after 10:00, most of which were caused by his insistence on working late; the work would be there tomorrow, as she pleaded with him, but he did not listen to her; nor did he even see the signs of her discontent until it was too late. Even when he was home, he was often too preoccupied with work or the bottles of beer that inhabited his refrigerator, the beers that helped him to forget, that he was still not spending proper time with his wife, or hearing her pleas to work on their marriage.

He spent many nights listening to others talk about the problems in their marriages, yet never took the time to appreciate the difficulties lurking within his until the date that he was served with a divorce complaint; the papers bore a format with which he was all too familiar, and when he was served with them he took them, numbly, as if they were just papers for another client.

The man walked out of Eric's office. He heard the man whisper something to the person in the adjacent room, and then heard the door slam as he exited the office. Eric knew that he would never see Steve Sanderson again. And that was fine with him. "I'll be out in a second," he called to the person whom he hoped was still waiting in the other room. He stood and peered out the window. The rain was intensifying and the sky was a dark black. The street lights cast an eerie glow about the buildings along Broad Street in downtown Elizabeth, including the courthouse which stood to the West. The sight of the courthouse mocked him.

Behind it lay a prison where the underbelly of Union County resided. To him, however, both his office and the courthouse, its rotunda lit up in the rainy night sky, were his prisons.

Perhaps one day he would see Steve Sanderson there, trying desperately to obtain a divorce on his own even though he had filed papers incorrectly. He would see Sanderson in the courtroom, being berated by a Judge for failing to file a required document, and hear the Judge tell the cheap bastard that he should retain counsel to do things properly. That also would be OK. Eric probably wouldn't recognize him, anyway. Steve was just one of the many people who came in and out of his office. There was no way that he could remember them all. Most he did not even want to remember.

CHAPTER II

The first thing that he noticed was her hair. As he crossed through the threshold of his office door into the next room, she was sitting in a chair, bent over, fumbling through the contents of an oversized pocketbook. As she looked down, her face was obscured by her long, curly hair. Most of the hair was a dark brown color, but there were lighter highlights throughout. Small droplets of water fell from the ends onto the carpet below, leading Eric to surmise that she had been caught in the rain which was now pelting the office windows like firecrackers.

He stared for what seemed like minutes as his visitor ran her hands, with their perfect painted fingernails, in and out of her bag, his gaze moving from the top of her head down to the legs which protruded underneath, crossed at the ankles and clad in tight black pants. He could glimpse a stripe of burgundy, the bottom inch or so of a blouse that sat atop and contrasted well with the dark black pants. Struggling to remember the name of his next appointment, Eric thought for a second before asking: "Ms. Rodrigues, I presume?"

Her head jerked up, more droplets of water flying in all directions as her waves and curls settled about her bare shoulders. Locks of hair fell forward, covering the top of her burgundy tank top and framing her cleavage. He could detect a slight tan line running inside of the tank top straps, further accentuating her obviously well-sized chest. "I'm sorry," she stammered in an accent quite familiar to a person who had spent the past fifteen years in Newark and Elizabeth, "I didn't see you there."

"Thank God," Eric thought, or she would have seen him staring at her. Bianca Rodrigues, Eric's 6:30 appointment, rose from her seat and extended her right hand. "No problem," he said, extending his hand to hers, "I was just finishing up with…"

"That *cuzao*? I'm sorry, that's my language, I mean that asshole?" she said, finishing Eric's sentence. "I heard what happened. You shouldn't have to put up with stuff like that, especially this late at night." Her Brazilian accent wafted through the room, filling Eric's head with visions of Rio and how Bianca would look clad in a bikini on its shores. When he didn't offer a response, she continued. "Thank you so much for meeting me this late at night," she said, scanning his office for pictures of a wife or children. "Don't you have a family to go home to?"

He again hesitated, his face no doubt belying the fact that he did not. "No," he answered, "not tonight. That's why I schedule clients back-to-back like this, so I can work late nights only once or twice a week." It was a lie, he realized, but he hoped that she did not think so. It was still best that his clients thought that he was married; a divorce attorney who was also divorced? The clients might think that he would be able to empathize with them, perhaps, but his feeling was that being a married man, more importantly, a family man, made him more attractive to clients. "Please, come in," he added before she asked any more questions about why he was still working as the clock approached 7:00, "it looks like the rain started a little too early for you."

"I know," she said as she walked past him into his office and settled into the leather chair, "I thought that I could get here before it started, but I was walking from the car on Broad Street when it really started to come down. And I forgot an umbrella, of course." She pushed the hair from her face, exposing more of her cleavage and the leopard-print bra which poked out from underneath her burgundy tank top. "My hair is a complete mess. I must look horrible."

"Don't be ridiculous," he answered, struggling to maintain his professionalism with a woman whom he had just met. "You look fine."

"Fine?" she asked, feigning insult. "Does your wife like it when you tell her that she looks fine, Mr. Goldberg?" She leaned forward, taking more of her hair in between the fingers of her left hand as her tank top strained, revealing even more of the leopard bra. The additional spots stared Eric in the face as he settled into his chair.

"I would say that she does not," he answered, remaining mindful of the fact that his lack of communication with his ex, like was the case with so many of his clients, directly led to the demise of his own marriage. He took the coffee cup from his desk and threw it into the garbage can to his left. "But this meeting is not about her, is it? We are here to talk about you. What brings you to this rainy part of Elizabeth tonight?"

Now it was Bianca who seemed uneasy. Her flirtatious nature gone, she placed her hands at her sides and began to explain the reasons why she had to be divorced from her husband. "We have been married for ten years," she said, eyes welling with tears, "since just after I came to this country. He was my first boyfriend here, and the only man who I have been with since I left Brazil." She paused and looked at Eric. "You know what I mean, right?"

"I think I do," replied Eric, struggling to avoid staring at her chest as they discussed her sex life with her soon-to-be ex-husband. "Let me ask you a couple of questions. How old are you now?"

"Thirty-one. And we have two children; one is ten and one is five. Both are girls." She noticed that he was not writing the information down on paper. "Shouldn't you be writing this down?" she asked.

"Not yet," he replied. "We are just going to talk first, and then see if it is something that we can pursue. If so, then I will take notes." She nodded in agreement, and Eric continued his line of questioning. "How old is he?"

"He's old. Forty-eight." She waited for a reaction, one that did not come. "Come on, Mr. Goldberg, you can say it. I was twenty-one when we were married. He was thirty-eight. You don't think that strange? Everyone from this country does." Now she sat back, waiting for Eric to make a comment about the age difference between her and her husband, the man whom she had married ten years ago because he made so much money, a man whom she came to realize that she had never loved, and with whom she shared a bed that felt like the fires of hell for the past decade. "You think I married him for his money, don't you?" She smiled and licked her lips like a lioness looking at her prey. "Young girl, older man. It had to be for the money, right?"

"Well, I don't think that forty-eight is all that old," Eric said, "I'm in my forties, so that's right around the corner. And you haven't told me what he does for a living, so I have no idea how much money he has or had when you were first married. And to tell you the truth," he said, leaning closer and lowering his voice even though nobody else was within earshot, "from what I've heard about Brazil, teenagers marrying older men is considered normal so I don't even think twice about it."

Now she was mad. Her eyes glowed and her body lurched forward. "How dare you," she shot back, "how dare you insult my country. Young girls get married all over the world, not just there." She stiffened, and crossed her arms in front of her ample chest. Her jaw tightened as she continued: "I thought that I loved him. I was young. What did I know?"

"That makes two of us," he thought to himself. He needed to bring the conversation back to an amicable tone. "I understand completely," he said calmly. "I am sure that you didn't just marry him for the money. But since we are on the topic, what exactly does your husband do for a living?"

She took a tissue from the box on the edge of Eric's desk and wiped the moisture from below her eyes, taking with it some of her mascara. "He is a contractor. He builds and does additions for houses. Walk around the Ironbound section in Newark, and he has fixed or built at least two houses on each street. He has also done lots of work in Elizabeth and Union County. Everyone knows him, his name is Joao Rodrigues." Eric's smile betrayed the fact that the name was familiar to him. "You know him?" she asked as he nodded his head, "I'm not surprised."

"He built a house that a client of mine bought once," Eric explained, "but to be honest with you, I wouldn't know him if I passed him in the street."

"Well, everything that we talk about is just between us, right?" she asked, "so you couldn't tell him anyway. But it's not like we're talking about anything bad," she paused, "at least not yet."

Eric was taken aback by the last part of her statement, and looked at her, puzzled, before continuing his questions. "Do you own a house together?"

"Yes, we do, in Union. It's a two-family house that we bought about seven years ago. There's no mortgage on it, to answer your next question, and I want to stay there with my kids. Can we do that?" she asked excitedly, her voice cracking, "Can I just make him move out? I can't live with him anymore. He tries to control me all of the time. He insults me, and tells me that I am worthless." She paused and took a deep breath. "He even says things like that in front of our children. Who does that?" Her tears began to flow anew.

"We can talk about that later," he said, moving his arms up and down slightly in an effort to calm her down and handing her another tissue. "Let me get some more information from you. What kind of insurance do you have?"

"You mean for doctors? I work in a doctor's office and we have insurance. My insurance is for all of us," she said, as she wiped the remaining tears from her cheeks. "We have insurance for the house and the car also, and he has life insurance, I think. Unless he got rid of it; last year he had about $2 million dollars in life insurance."

"Worth more dead than alive, I guess," Eric joked, but Bianca did not smile. "I assume you are the beneficiary of the policy, if he still has it."

"Maybe," she said, the lilt returning to her voice, "I really don't know. I would hope that it is me or the kids. Maybe I will have to kill him just to find out."

"That seems a bit extreme to me, wouldn't you say?" he replied, looking to see if she was merely trying to amuse herself. "Let's talk about cost and procedure, if you don't mind." He discussed the financial aspects of a divorce matter, his hourly rate, the monies that he would need to begin, and the anticipated time between the initial filing of the complaint and the actual granting of the divorce on her behalf.

She thought about the information, about the money and time, and about the manner in which Eric had presented both himself and his ability to properly handle her case. "I won't yell at you like the last guy," she said, chuckling lightly, "but the money you are saying is a little high. I don't know if I can get that much now. Do you offer payment plans?" She again leaned forward and showcased her breasts, which by now it was clear to Eric was her way of asking for favors.

"Sorry, but no," he said, averting his gaze and turning to the window. "I have had problems with people paying me in the past, so I try to avoid having those problems now whenever possible. I think you will find that I am worth the money if you give me a try." He almost bit his tongue as the words exited his mouth, realizing the double entendre contained within his otherwise innocuous yet clearly self-aggrandizing comment. Changing the subject, he added: "listen to that rain coming down. It sounds like it's harder than they said it would be."

"The rain is peaceful," she said, "and being peaceful is not often for me now. *Me faz lembrar minha casa*, it reminds me of home, back in Brazil. It is never peaceful in my house here, and it will not be peaceful until I get rid of him. I will get the money. Then I can come back and we can start, right?"

She stood and then bent over to pick up her bag, this time placing her firm backside directly in Eric's view. She stayed in the position for a full minute, explaining that she was looking for a piece of paper on which to write the stated fees, before she straightened up, running her right hand along the side of her obviously well-toned leg as she stood. Extending the same hand to Eric, she thanked him for his time and told him that she would be in touch. She turned to the door, but stopped in response to Eric's words.

"The rain is really hard," he said, "please take my umbrella."

"But then you will get wet," she answered, "I will feel badly knowing that you are walking to your car in the rain. I normally carry an umbrella in my car, but I took my husband's van tonight. But I'll be OK. What's the worst that can happen, my clothes get wet?"

That would be far from the worst thing, Eric thought. In fact, that would be the vision that would stay with him for the remainder of the night, whether or not it actually came to pass. "I insist, Bianca, please take the umbrella. You say that you'll be back. When you come back, you can bring the umbrella with you. I'm only parked a block away, so it's not a long walk anyway. Take it." He paused, and then handed her his black umbrella, adding, "besides, this way you have to come back. Look inside the umbrella. Underneath – my name is written in silver ink, see where it says E. Goldberg? This way you will know that it is mine and that you have to come back to return it to me."

"Thank you," she said, leaning toward him and kissing him lightly on both cheeks. "You are a very nice man, Mr. Goldberg. I will see you soon." She turned and walked away, no doubt aware of the fact that Eric's eyes burned two holes in her ass as she strutted out the door. Eric followed her, closed the door behind him, and slumped down in the leather chair which still smelled of Bianca. Her smell and the vision of her walking away eased the disappointment of another evening, an evening of appointments which, as yet, did yield even one money-making case.

There were no more excuses to avoid going home to his empty apartment. It was now 7:30. His dog would no doubt have to be fed and walked. Eric took a folder from a stack of supplies below his photocopy machine to shield his hair from the rain, turned off the office lights, locked the door behind him and walked to the elevator. His steps echoed through the otherwise empty hallway, the same echoes which would greet him in the hallways of his own apartment.

CHAPTER III

Bianca Rodrigues arrived home just as the clock in her car turned to 8:15. She had stopped on the way home at the Shop Rite on Morris Avenue in Union, slowly winding her way through the narrow aisles of the dimly-lit, dingy supermarket as she tried to determine what she would make for dinner that evening.

Looking at the feeble selection of fresh fish that remained in the semi-melted ice at the seafood counter, she decided that she did not feel like cooking that night, instead deciding to pick up some Portuguese Rolls and cold cuts. Moving to the deli counter, she ordered a half-pound each of salami, ham, and cheese. Putting the meats and cheese into the basket in her hand, she also picked up some spices and rice on her way back to the checkout line. Again having forgotten the umbrella, she ran through the parking lot to her car, carrying her two shopping bags, the puddles which had accumulated in the decrepit parking lot forcing mini-torrents of water up over her shoes and the bottoms of her pants legs.

As she walked through the door into her house from the garage, she called to her daughters to take the groceries from her and, removing her shoes, walked with wet feet to her bedroom. Sitting on the toilet in her bathroom, she reached down and felt the soaked bottoms of her pants legs. Realizing that they would remain wet and uncomfortable for the remainder of the evening, she removed her pants and laid them over the edge of the bathroom's soaking tub. Reaching for the shorts that lay on the other side of the tub, the shorts that she had worn to bed the previous night, she looked back and caught a glimpse of her rear end in the mirror. She stopped, still looking backward, and considered her thong-clad rear, which she considered to be impressive. She lay the shorts back down on the tub edge, and pulled her tank top down so that it reached to the tops of her thighs. Again admiring herself in the mirror, she decided that she did not need to put on any other pants and instead strode to the kitchen clad only in her tank top, which was now showing more of the leopard-print bra, and her black thong, which poked out from underneath the tank top, along with the bottom of her ass, as she walked.

Carla, her older daughter, took one look at her as she entered the kitchen and rolled her eyes in exasperation. "Come on, mom," she pleaded, "go put some pants on. You're so embarrassing. People can see in through the windows," she added, pointing outside.

"*Não se incomode com os outros.* Don't worry about others, Carla," Bianca answered, "nobody can see in here. And besides, it is pouring outside. Who will be outside looking in now?" Actually, there was one person that she could think of - her next door neighbor, Steve Moore, who had a strange but well-defined habit of taking his garbage out to the cans in between the two houses whenever Bianca arrived home. She derived excitement from the fact that he watched her, though, so that was not a reason for her to cover up. In reality, it was more of a reason to stay dressed as she was. She reached into the wet shopping bag on the kitchen table, picked up the bag of rice that she had just purchased, and, then reached up to open the cabinet and put the rice away on its proper shelf. As she reached up, her tank top also rose, so that the bottom of the tank top was now a full inch above the top of her black thong. She could feel the cold of the a/c-cooled air on her lower back, which was now slightly arched as she leaned against the kitchen counter, and she wondered if her neighbor was watching from outside.

"Mom, seriously!" her daughter shrieked as she saw her mother's perfectly-formed and thong-clad rear just inches from the kitchen window. "Can you please act like an adult and put some clothes on?"

Bianca placed the rice into the cabinet and turned, the front of her black thong now staring her daughter in the face. Pulling down her tank top again so that the entirety of the black fabric was concealed beneath the burgundy tank top, Bianca asked, "is this good enough for you?" Turning to the side as if modeling the shirt for her daughter, she kept both hands on the hem of the tank top to prevent it from riding up the sides of her legs. "Now get your sister in here and let's have dinner." The three ate sandwiches for dinner, the girls sitting at the kitchen table and Bianca leaning against the stainless steel edge of the sink, the feel of the cold metal stimulating the bare tops of her thighs.

After dinner the girls went to their respective rooms, Carla to check her facebook on the computer and Leila to get ready for bed. Bianca cleared the table, putting the dishes and glasses in the sink. She was about to go into her husband's home office, to retrieve the papers that she needed for her next meeting with her new attorney, when she glanced to the right and saw, through the kitchen window, Steve Moore slowly putting a bag of garbage into the large can which sat next to his house. His eyes glistened in the rain-soaked night, and Bianca could tell that he was looking through the window at her. Seeing her looking at him, he quickly averted his eyes downward to the can. And he stood there for the next few seconds, not moving.

Bianca slowly opened the dishwasher to her left and began to place the glasses on its top rack. Each time that she placed a glass into the dishwasher, the bottom of her tank top crept ever so slightly up the back of her thighs. By the time that the third glass was in the dishwasher, the bottom of her ass was poking out from underneath the shirt, and Bianca carefully avoided looking outside so as not to force Steve Moore to look away.

She imagined him looking at her, becoming aroused as he stood like a sentinel at his garbage can, his gaze fixed on her legs and butt as she started to place the dishes on the bottom rack of the dishwasher. The vision of Steve Moore becoming aroused excited her, and she could feel the pores on her body begin to harden both from her excitement and the air flowing from the air conditioner.

She took a plate and, in an exaggerated motion, she bent downward, from the waist, to place it at the back of the bottom rack. The bottom hem of the tank top leapt to her midsection, and she slowly moved her legs back and forth to show off her thong to her no-doubt entranced neighbor. Again standing, she did not make any attempt to fix her shirt as she took another plate and again bent over to place it into the dishwasher.

As she stood this time, she glanced to the right and saw Steve Moore quickly turn and walk swiftly to his house's side door. While she couldn't be sure, she thought that she saw the fabric of his shorts straining in front.

Placing the last plate into the dishwasher, she dried her hands, closed the dishwasher, and fixed her tank top so that it again reached to her thighs. She strode to her husband's office, and began to rifle through his desk and cabinet to find the necessary documents. She was sitting in his chair, the cool leather sticking to her thighs, when she found the house deed and last mortgage statement. She also was able to locate the last statements from two different investment accounts that she did not even know existed; one of which was in both of their names and one of which was in his name alone. She was looking over that statement when her younger daughter appeared. "Mommy, I want to go to bed. Can you tuck me in?"

"*Claro.* Of course I will," Bianca replied, standing and walking toward her daughter, "let's go to your room. Did you brush your teeth?"

"Of course I did, mommy," Leila said, mimicking her mother's statement as she climbed into bed. Pulling the blanket up to her neck, she looked up and said, "and I don't care what Carla said, mommy, I think you look beautiful tonight."

Tears welled in Bianca's eyes as she bent down to kiss Leila goodnight. "*Obrigada, bebê.* Thank you, baby," Bianca said softly, "and you are my precious and beautiful angel. *Boa noite.* Good night. I will see you in the morning." She kissed Leila on the forehead, stood, and switched off the light. Closing the door behind her as she exited the room, she told her daughter that she loved her, saying, in whispered Portuguese, "*a mamãe te ama.*"

"I love you, too, mommy," answered Leila, as she rolled over and closed her eyes to sleep.

Drying the tears from her eyes, Bianca walked to her other daughter's room and opened the door without knocking. Carla sat on her bed, computer propped on her lap as she furiously typed notes to her various friends. Covering the computer screen with her hands as her mother approached, she angrily said, "Mom! Don't you knock before you come in? I'm busy."

"It's my house," Bianca answered, "so I knock when I want to. Are you on Facebook again? I know it is summer, but can't you read or do something better than that?" She leaned in to see the screen through her daughter's fingers. She could see the omnipresent blue banner of Facebook, and various small pictures of pre-teenage girls along the whole left side of the page. Straightening up, the bottom of her black thong again exposed and close to her daughter's horrified face, she said, "alright, do what you want. But only for another half hour. Then I want you to go to bed." Her daughter protested, to which Bianca replied, sternly, "another half hour. If I come in here after that and you are still on the computer, I am taking it away." She walked away, closed the door behind her, and returned to the office.

Again sitting down in the leather chair, she glanced at the clock on the desk, which read 9:30. She could barely hear the phone ring as she shuffled through the papers in each of the desk drawers, so focused on finding anything new that she did not hear her daughter enter the room. "Mom," her elder daughter said, "dad's on the phone." Bianca stood to take the phone from her daughter, her shirt again riding up to her midsection. Cupping the phone in her left hand and covering her eyes with her right, an exasperated Carla handed the phone to her mother.

Taking the phone and covering the mouthpiece with her own hand, Bianca looked at her daughter's grimace and the hand over her eyes and said, coldly, "grow up, Carla. You should be so lucky to look this good when you are my age." She waved her other hand in the air. "Now go to bed." Seeing her daughter begin to protest, she added, "OK, facebook for a little while more, then bed, OK?" Her daughter nodded and smiled, hand still covering her eyes, as she turned and left the room.

"Hello," she said into the phone, "*onde você está* (where are you), Joao?" She could head the rushing wind through the phone, clearly indicating that her husband was driving as they spoke. "It's 9:30. When are you going to be home?"

"In a little while," he answered, "I have to meet some people about work stuff and then I will be there. About 10:30. Don't worry about food for me, I ate before."

"At 10:30 I don't worry about food for you," she said, "the girls and I already had dinner. Just come home," she added as she clicked off the phone.

Now she only had a little more than an hour to find all of the papers. She knew that he would never be home by 10:30, as promised, but if he was only a half hour late that still only gave her until 11:00. She ran her fingers over the tops of each of the papers in the desk and adjacent file cabinet, searching for anything that she could use or did not recognize.

Suddenly, she stopped. Peering more carefully at the sheet of paper in the cabinet, she could see that it was a hotel receipt, a receipt from a hotel in Asbury Park. It was dated earlier in June, about a week ago, but she hadn't gone to Asbury Park within the last couple of weeks. Neither did Joao, to her knowledge. The only thing that he had done was to go to the Yankees' game with his friends, and then, he told her, he stayed at one of their houses so that he did not come home too late to wake the girls.

At least that was what he said. He must have been with one of them, she thought, as she took the receipt and placed it on the desk on top of the house papers. She also found several other receipts, including one for a pair of diamond earrings that somehow never made it to her earlobes. She stewed silently as she placed paper after paper on top of the others, each paper confirming the suspicions that she had harbored for years about her husband's infidelity.

In the last drawer, she also found insurance papers, which showed that Joao had over two million dollars in life insurance spread over three policies. One policy was for $250,000 and the girls were the beneficiaries. Bianca was the beneficiary on all of the other policies. Each policy also had a paid receipt attached to it, showing that they were paid in full only five months earlier so Bianca assumed that they were all still valid. Gathering up these papers with the others on the desk, she carefully closed all of the drawers and put everything back into its place so that Joao would not know that she had even been in there. She would make copies the next day and put everything back, she reasoned, and he would be none the wiser.

Returning to the living room, Bianca curled up on the couch, reached for the remote control, and turned on the television. In front of her, partially-closed curtains adorned the room's large bay window, and the only light in the living room, situated at the front of the house, came from the glow of the television and light from the street lamp which made its way through the opening in between curtains. Her head resting against a pillow as she tried to put her rage against her husband aside for a short while, she pulled her legs up to her midsection as she watched a rerun of "Chopped" on Food Network. She had the sound up just loud enough that she could hear it, but it was low enough that it would not wake her sleeping daughters or bother her tenants, the upstairs neighbors.

The "Chopped" contestants were well into making their main course, struggling to fashion meals out of a basket of ingredients completely foreign to Bianca, when she heard her husband's car on the driveway. She heard the car door open and shut, and the muffled sounds of two men talking. The clock read 10:25. She rose and walked toward the kitchen, peering around the corner so that she could see outside but that she could not be seen. There she saw her husband talking to Steve Moore, who was putting out yet another bag of garbage (and no doubt disappointed that he had seen Joao and not Bianca, she presumed). She returned to her seat on the couch as the "Chopped" judges were critiquing the competitors' offerings. The side door opened, and Bianca's husband stepped into the room and turned on the lights.

"What are you watching?" he asked, loudly. *"O que você está assistindo?"* he repeated, walking toward the back of the couch where all that he could see was the top of her head. "Another one of these stupid cooking shows?"

Bianca, already poised and ready for a fight with her cheating husband, jumped off of the couch and stood in front of him, bathed in the light of the television. Her tank top rested atop the upper part of her pelvic bone, the black color of her thong shining in the television's glow. *"Por que você se preocupa* (Why do you care)?" she demanded, "you don't even come home until 10:30 at night, so why do you care what I do?" Her voice was strong but low, so as not to wake the children.

Glancing at the open curtains behind his wife, Joao responded, "I was out working, that's why I care. I don't see you with a job." He moved closer, to the back side of the couch. "Is this what you do all day, sit and watch TV in your underwear? *Va colocar uma roupa, sua prostituta.*"

Bianca glared at her husband. *"O que você disse?"* she replied, "what did you say to me?"

"You heard me," said her husband, in an accusing tone. "Put on some clothes, you whore. People can see your ass through the window." He reached for the TV remote on the couch, but Bianca quickly reached down and grabbed it before he could reach it.

"*Prostituta*? You call me a whore?" she cried, throwing the TV remote to the floor. "Am I any more of a *prostituta* than any of those women you run around with?" It was the first time that she had ever confronted him with the fact that she knew of his affairs, and she waited for his response. She expected rage. She was not surprised.

"What the fuck are you talking about?" he bellowed. She motioned to him to be quiet so that he did not wake the children, but his voice remained raised. "Run around with? I don't know what you are talking about!"

"I know all about it. *Eu ja sei há anos.*" She began to sob. "I've known for years. It got to the point where I couldn't even walk around the neighborhood without thinking that people were looking at me, laughing at me, because they knew that you were fucking around."

She looked at him. "What happened to me that made you go to other women?" she asked plaintively. She grabbed the bottom hem of her tank top with both hands, quickly lifted it up over her head, and threw it, in a heap, onto the couch. Now she stood, in the light of the room and in front of the partially-opened blinds, clad only her in leopard-print bra and black thong panties. "Am I not attractive to you anymore?" she asked, as she ran her hands through her tousled hair.

He looked at her almost-naked body, then looked away and turned to leave the room. "You're not attractive to me at all. Besides, *eu sou apenas uma carteira para você* (I'm just a wallet to you). *Você me dá nojo* (You disgust me), you whore," he said, as he walked to his office. "*Vá ficar nua enfrente a janela.* Go stand naked in front of the window," he added, "maybe one of the neighbors wants to watch your little show. *Estou cansado disso tudo.*"

"You're sick of it?" she yelled. "Is that what you just said to me?" She again started to cry, pulling her arms in front of her to shield her body. "I saw a lawyer today," she yelled. "*Vou divorciar de você.* I'm going to divorce you. I don't need to live like this anymore." She ran to his office, where he was sitting in the chair that she had occupied only an hour before. "And one other thing, you *porco*. I'm taking your daughters from you. If it is up to me, *você nunca as vera novamente.*"

"Stupid whore," he called, "don't make threats that you can't keep. Of course I will see them again. I am their father." He laughed, as if he knew a secret of which she was ignorant. "In fact, *meu amor*," he said sarcastically as he stood, the glow of his desk lamp bathing him in a threatening aura, "*Vamos ver quem fica com a guarda delas.*" He then repeated his threat in English. "Let's see who gets custody of them."

Bianca had never even considered the possibility that he would fight her for custody of the girls. He was never even home. "Why would you fight me for custody? You never even spend time with them?" she yelled.

"*É facil*," he replied. "That's easy. Because it would hurt you, you ungrateful, pathetic, whore."

Bianca picked up the remote control from the floor and ran toward her husband, arm raised as if she intended to strike him with the object. Halfway to him, however, she stopped, not wanting to receive the brunt of his response as she saw him start to walk out from behind his desk to confront her. "*Você nunca vai tirar minhas filhas de mim.* You will never take my children from me," she cried, turning and fleeing from the room. She ran to her bedroom, locked the door behind her, and collapsed, sobbing, on her bed.

CHAPTER IV

Eric's son, Jason, did not come home that night. Eric received a text message while walking to his car in the rain: "Dad – not coming home – staying at Jon's." Facing another night alone, Eric strode to the Burger King on the corner of Broad Street and Dickinson, wiped the raindrops off of his suit, and proceeded to order a Whopper, fries, and soda to go. He had not been to the Burger King for at least three months; the last time had been just before his divorce was finalized. Since that time, he had been trying to eat healthier, and the first thing that he had tried to eliminate from his diet was fast food.

Up until this night, he had been successful. The girl behind the counter handed him a bag containing the burger and fries, along with the cup of soda. He walked to the side counter, took a straw and napkins, and steeled himself for the rainy night. Running the last half-block to his car while protecting his food and drink, he failed to notice the giant puddle alongside the curb and, when he finally reached his car, he did so with a left fairly-wet and spotted light brown shoe and a dark brown, soaking wet shoe on his right foot.

He arrived home that night, strolling to the kitchen as his wet shoe made damp impressions along the hallway and foyer in his apartment. Without changing his clothes, he returned outside and walked Peyton, his beagle, for an additional ten minutes in the now slowing rains. Returning inside, he vigorously rubbed a towel over Peyton to dry his fur, removed his suit, shirt, and tie and threw them into a rumpled ball in the corner of his bathroom, and threw his shoes into his bathroom sink. He put on a pair of running shorts and his favorite Colts' football jersey, and sat down on his couch to eat his dinner.

The Big Mac was, not surprisingly, cold and wet from the journey home and the time that had elapsed since he had purchased it from the Burger King. It had semi-coagulated cheese on it, making him regret saying "no cheese" and not "no queso" to the Hispanic girl who took his order. The fries were limp and cold. The outside of the soda cup was drenched, both with rain and condensation, and the bottom of the cup felt so loose that Eric thought that it would burst any second. He poured the soda, with its little remaining ice, into a glass that he pulled from his cupboard.

Walking back to the couch, he turned on the television, and found a baseball game to watch. He sat back down on the couch, ripped off a piece of the burger and threw it to Peyton, and then proceeded to eat, in undesired solitude, the remainder of his cold, wet dinner.

As there wasn't much other food in the apartment, he rationalized, he didn't have much choice. He was sad, however, as he sat there alone, wishing that his son had come home to join him.

Following a night marked by only three hours of consecutive sleep, Eric rose at 6:15am and walked to the bathroom to take a shower, the sounds of raindrops continuing to slap at the small window which served as both light source and ventilation for his bathroom. After a hot shower, he stepped into the steamy bathroom, wiped an area in the middle of the mirror hanging over the sink, and ran his electric razor over his cheeks and neck, being careful to leave the rectangle of hair that comprised his goatee. Wiping any excess water from his face and neck, he dressed in a navy suit, pale yellow shirt, and gold-and-navy striped repp tie. He took Peyton for a quick walk, this time remembering to carry an umbrella to shield them both from the rain that had pelted the area for the past twelve hours, then walked back into the apartment, placed the dog's food into his bowl, and left for a new day at the office.

He arrived at the office at 7:30. Quickly glancing at the calendar on his computer, he noted that his first appointment for the day was not scheduled until 10:00am, which he understood to mean that the first person would not be coming in to the office until approximately 10:30 or so. This gave him three hours to complete whatever work he desired before that first visitor.

He switched his internet browser to ESPN, his home page, to check the baseball scores and news from the night before. He first checked his fantasy baseball team, which continued to be mired in sixth place out of the ten teams in the league.

"Disgraceful," he muttered to himself, as he clicked to the previous night's scores. There he saw that his favorite team, the New York Yankees, had suffered a 6-2 defeat at the hands of the lowly Seattle Mariners.

It was the Yankees' seventh loss in their last ten games, and had dropped them into third place, behind the Toronto Blue Jays and the Baltimore Orioles. There was still plenty of baseball left to be played in the season, but the local media was already declaring the Yankees' season to be over. In reading the article and the account of the haplessness of the vaunted Yankee offense against the rookie Seattle pitcher the night before, Eric was in no position to disagree.

Eric spent the next hour returning e-mails from the previous afternoon and evening. None were overly urgent, other than to the senders who always believed that their work was more important than everyone else's, but he reasoned that it was better to deal with the correspondences instead of waiting for their writers to call the office and demand responses. As he would tell people, there's not much nice that can be said about the person who sends an e-mail at 8:00pm and then calls the next morning at 9:05 demanding an answer. That person needs to be shown that the world does not always work according to their schedule.

Today, however, was not the day for Eric to be teaching that lesson. His head hurt from a lack of sleep the previous night –

the throbbing in his temples was rhythmic, ironically not unlike the driving beat of Frankie Goes to Hollywood's classic *"Relax"*, and the last thing that he wanted was to engage in any arguments with irate clients or adversaries. Far better to simply dash off quick responses to those who had felt the need to correspond in the middle of the night; this way, he could avoid their phone calls on the premise that he had already provided his responses to them.

Shuffling through some of the papers which littered his desk, Eric came across a letter from his adversary on a case which was scheduled for a hearing the following Friday. Contained within the two pages of the letter were no less than ten allegations of infidelity and lying against Eric's client, Jean Masters. He wondered to himself how many of the allegations were true. About six or seven, he guessed, not that it mattered anyway. He would go to court as if all of the statements were false, and do his best to force the judge to question everything that his client's soon-to-be-ex-husband would say. He started to make notes on the paper, struggling to keep his writing neat enough so that he could quickly read it while in the courtroom.

The silence was broken by the sound of the phone ringing. Eric glanced over at the clock on his desk, which now read 8:55. He decided not to answer the phone – it was too early to deal with anyone's problems, he reasoned, and if it was important enough they would leave a message and he could return it at his own leisure. He finished making his notations on his adversary's letter just as the door to his office opened.

"Good morning" called out a familiar voice.

"If you say so, Fatima," he replied while searching the file cabinet next to his desk for the Masters file, "has it stopped raining yet?"

"Wish that it had," Fatima Esteves Goldberg replied, as she carefully placed a wet cup of coffee on Eric's desk, atop the sticky ring which signified coffee cups past. Drops of water shone on her hair. "I thought it was supposed to be done by today, but who knows. And stupid me had to go get coffee; you would think that walking in the rain alone would wake me up," she laughed, "but apparently such an assumption would be wrong. And I knew that you wouldn't drag your lazy ass to the coffee shop. You haven't bought coffee in the morning since they closed the Dunkin' Donuts across from the courthouse." Fatima had been Eric's assistant for six years. She had been his cousin's wife for six years and two weeks. They had met at Fatima's wedding to Eric's cousin, Bruce Goldberg.

Maria Fatima Esteves, who preferred, like many others with her name, to go by the name Fatima, was born in Newark's Ironbound section, the middle daughter of Portuguese immigrants. The Ironbound section of Newark, known as "down neck" to its residents, had gained national attention during the Newark riots of the mid-1960's. At a time when Newark and other urban areas in the United States were under siege by their African-American inhabitants, the European-born residents of the Ironbound, nestled between Penn Station and railroad tracks to the West and factories and the Atlantic Ocean to the East, stood at the edge of their neighborhood, armed with baseball bats, and dared the rioters to enter their section of the city. None did.

At a time when "white flight" resulted from Europeans, Jews, and other whites fleeing the city in the 60's and 70's for the burgeoning suburbs to the west, the Portuguese remained in the Ironbound, to be joined in their homes up and down Ferry and Market Streets by the similar-speaking Brazilians.

Her father worked in construction, and her mother spent her days working in a local supermarket. Fatima and her sisters were raised in Newark, spending most of their time interacting with other Portuguese and Brazilians in the city's section best known for its Portuguese-speaking inhabitants and world-class restaurants.

Like many others, she spoke only Portuguese at home until she went to school, but she quickly picked up English and Spanish as well and graduated from East Side High School in the top ten percent of her class. After one semester at Seton Hall University in South Orange, however, her father was severely injured in a workplace accident and his disability payments were not sufficient, along with her mother's salary, to cover the family's expenses.

Fatima decided to leave school and went to work as a receptionist in a local realtor's office on Ferry Street.

Some time later, at a friend's party, she was introduced to Bruce Goldberg. He was five years her senior, a graduate of the University of Pittsburgh, and had returned home to New Jersey to work as a manager for his father's company. While he had never intended to work with his family, he was making use of his Bachelor's degree in business to increase sales and generate revenues higher than ever before.

Far from being just the "boss' son", he had established himself amongst the other employees as a valuable player in the company's fortunes. He was five feet ten inches tall, about seven inches taller than her, and his dark brown hair was the same color as Fatima's, more appropriately, it was the same color as Fatima's before she added layers of highlights, which now made her hair a veritable spectrum of auburns and browns. They were immediately drawn to each other, and began dating in earnest only a few weeks later.

Within a year, Fatima had converted to Judaism and they were married. The wedding was the first time that she had met several members of Bruce's extended family, including Eric. At the time she was looking for a job and Eric had just lost his secretary. The two talked briefly at the wedding, and then more when she returned from her honeymoon in Jamaica. The law was something in which Fatima had always been interested, and despite her trepidation about working for family she accepted Eric's offer of employment.

Now, six years later, she joked that she had actually married two cousins – her real husband, Bruce, and her work husband, Eric. The bond between Eric and Fatima, both liked to say, was more than just a relationship between co-workers. They were family, and each cared deeply for and tried to take care of each other. Lately, however, Fatima's need to "mother" Eric had increased dramatically, especially since his divorce was finalized.

"You look like shit," she added, looking at the bags under Eric's eyes and the red lines which ran like spiderwebs outward from his corneas. "Did you get any sleep last night?"

He shook his head slowly and looked toward the window. "Can't say that I really did. I don't know why, but it was just one of those nights." He turned his head to her. "You know, the usual. I did sleep for a couple of hours here and there, but nothing consistent." He reached for the coffee and pushed back the lid. "Thanks for the coffee. Lord knows I need it this morning."

"Did the people at least come in last night?" she asked, "did we get any new clients?" He liked it when she used words like "we" and "us" when describing his work. It didn't sound at all presumptuous to him. Rather, he appreciated how she considered the firm to be her business as well as his, and that she treated her work so seriously. She looked him directly in the eye. "Did she come in?"

His eyes widened, the red lines becoming more evident. "What do you mean, did she come in?"

"You know exactly what I mean," she responded, "did Bianca come in?"

"Bianca?" Eric asked with a sarcastic tone in his voice, "should I take it that you two are now on a first name basis?" Of course, he immediately knew the answer to that question. One thing about the Ironbound neighborhood where Fatima was raised is that everyone knew each other. Whether they were Portuguese or Brazilian, everybody knew someone who knew everybody else. And everyone therefore knew everyone else's business.

This was especially true when there was a scandal involved. Several years earlier, boxer Arturo Gatti was found dead and his Brazilian wife, Amanda Rodrigues, was the prime suspect. One of Fatima's best friends was good friends with Amanda – and regaled Fatima and Bruce with tales of the beatings that Arturo would inflict on his wife, tales of the black eyes, bruised lips, and a multitude of reasons why it would have been justifiable if Amanda had actually killed her husband. As her trial went on both in the courts and in the court of public opinion, there was nary a person in the area who did not have a perspective of their own, often based not on the alleged facts of the case, but rather on their own personal, or someone else's, past dealings with her.

"You know that I know them, stupid," she replied, "I know her husband. I don't know her personally, but I have heard stories. She's bad, from what I hear. Be careful around her. You know how those Brazilian women can be," she said sternly as she made direct eye contact with Eric for the first time during their conversation, stressing the last sentence to make sure that he understood her words of caution.

The other thing about the mix of Portuguese and Brazilians is that they really do not like each other too much; their relationship is now based more on jealousy, as it had been explained to Eric on numerous occasions, with the Portuguese being jealous of the fact that the Brazilians outnumber them by the millions and the fact that the Brazilians have bastardized their language to the extent that the Brazilian form of the Portuguese language is now more recognized in most places than its continental counterpart. The Portuguese also detest that the Brazilian soccer team is light years more accomplished than their own.

On the other side, as he was told, the Brazilians have difficulty with the fact that the Portuguese consider them to be lazy, especially when the Brazilian economy has become one of the world leaders while the Portuguese economy teeters on the edge of destruction. The Brazilians resent that the Portuguese still consider them to be like a little brother, a belief which has no merit now due to the relative positions of the two countries in size, population, and gross domestic profit.

"Yes," he laughed, "she came in. You're not going to preach to me now, are you?" He leaned forward. "She was very nice. Why don't you tell me all of the horrible things that you have heard about her so that I know what to look for when she comes back?"

"When she comes back? Don't you mean if?"

"No," Eric said firmly, "I mean when. I was good last night. I was charming. I was smart. I don't care how much you know her husband or whether you think that she is bad and he is a paragon of goodness and virtue. Mark my words, we will represent her on her divorce. I got a vibe from her."

Now it was Fatima's turn to laugh. "A vibe," she chuckled. "what are you, in high school?" She paused and leaned forward, her hands now resting on the edge of Eric's desk. "That's what she does, you asshole. She uses men. She flirts with them, makes them feel special. And then she takes things from them. Believe me, whatever she told you, believe the opposite. I am not saying that her husband is perfect." She straightened up and saw the look of doubt on Eric's face. "And no, the fact that he is Portuguese has nothing to do with it," she stammered as she turned and walked out of the room. Eric heard her slam her chair against the wall, no doubt by accident, and the sound of her fingers angrily typing as he leaned back in his chair, closed his eyes, and tried as hard as he could to remember every detail of his meeting with Bianca. What he could remember best, of course, was the tank top and the breasts and leopard-print bra that were doing their best to break free.

CHAPTER V

At approximately 10:15, Eric was struggling to prepare interrogatory answers for a client when the phone rang. Fatima answered before it rang a second time, and he could not hear her side of the conversation, although he could tell that her tone was not overly friendly. He wondered which client had called after she hung up the phone, and what that person could have said to annoy her. He was about to call out to her when she appeared in his doorway. "It was her," she said coldly, "she wants to come in again to see you today."

Eric feigned a lack of understanding as to whom Fatima was referring. "She?" he questioned, "who is she?" A small smile creased his face.

Fatima noticed the smile immediately. "You know exactly who I mean. Wipe that smirk off your face." She walked toward him, around to the back of his desk, and stood, her own ample chest inches from his face. "Is this what she did last night?" she asked, leaning toward him, the scoop neck of her floral print dress exposing the tops of her breasts and cleavage, "is this how she explained her troubles to you?"

Eric quickly reached around her waist with his left hand, and pulled her size-14 dress and body closer to him so that his face nestled slightly within the cleavage of her breasts, his nose resting softly atop the hem of her dress. The warm bursts of air from

Eric's nose made the pores in between Fatima's breasts stiffen, and he imagined that her nipples were hardening, although imperceptibly, beneath the thick cloth bra that lay underneath the flowers which encircled her chest. "Come on Maria," he said, using the first name that she so hated, "it wasn't like that at all. And another thing," he said, pausing, before forcing another hot breath down the top of her dress, "my cousin is a lucky guy." His voice was muffled by the fabric of her dress, and she quickly put her hands on his shoulders in an attempt to free his grasp. As she torqued her body backward, Eric's hand slid, involuntarily, down from her waist along the outside of her left butt cheek, slightly pulling at the fabric and exposing more of her left thigh.

She stepped backward, her anger obvious. She was angry not at the fact that he had grabbed her, which, for reasons that she could not explain and would never tell anyone about, excited her slightly. Rather, she was enraged at the fact that he was not listening to her. In her mind, she was his new moral compass. She was his only "wife" now, and was the only person who could try, although usually unsuccessfully, to keep him in line.

Her face flustered both with rage and from the light sensation of Eric's hand having gently caressed her backside, she said, sternly, as she ran her hands in a quick up-and-down motion from her chest to the top of her legs, "this is exactly what I am talking about. This, what you just did, you can't do that shit with her. It will get you in trouble. I know how you are," she glared at him, "I know how you are with the women, especially the attractive women. Don't do it with her, I am warning you, it will only be bad." Her eyes were like daggers, the brown pupils flashing red in a color scheme which almost perfectly matched her hair.

Eric stood up, warily, and placed his left hand on her right shoulder. Squeezing her shoulder lightly, he responded, "Don't worry. I've got this. First of all, I'm not going to let anything happen so you shouldn't be jealous." He looked at her face, searching for a semblance of amity, but noted none. "Second of all, it's a business thing. We need the work. We both need the money. If I just said no to clients because one of us didn't like them," he said as he pulled his hand from her shoulder, "we would have a lot of free time on our hands."

Clearly not pleased by the response, Fatima turned to walk back to her desk. As she turned, the bottom hem of her dress flew slightly to the right, again baring the upper part of her right thigh. "One more thing, Fatima," Eric said as she turned back to listen, "your ass felt pretty good. Have you been working out?"

"Fuck you," she responded as she again turned away. She began to walk slowly from the room, slightly accentuating her gait as she swiveled her hips from side to side. "Yes, I have been," she added, "eat your fucking heart out." She stopped, and again turned back around so that she faced Eric, her stance enhancing her profile so that her head was within the doorway but her breasts were in the next room, "and by the way, she will be here at two. Just try to keep it in your pants, for the sake of both of us."

2:00 pm came and went with no sign of Bianca. The rain continued to fall outside, the office phones were silent, and Eric sat as his desk, absent-mindedly typing corrections to a letter that he had written earlier that day. He glanced down at the clock on the lower right-hand corner of his computer screen continuously, watching the "minute" numbers grow as his anticipation for his client's visit heightened. He tried to imagine what she would be wearing. No doubt something sexy, he thought, and if Fatima was right about Bianca and her flirtatious nature, then it would be exceptionally sexy. And he found that possibility to be more than acceptable.

The number on the computer showed 2:21 when Eric heard the office door open. He heard the muffled sound of two women talking; while he could not make out the specific words, it was clear that one of the women was Fatima, as he recognized the cadence of her voice. The conversation did not appear to be an overly amiable one based on what he could make out, so he assumed that Bianca had finally arrived for her appointment. He glanced toward the door separating his room from the rest of the office, and Fatima's face appeared. "She's here," Fatima said coldly, and then she looked him in the eye and mouthed "remember what I said. Don't do anything stupid."

Eric rose from his chair, whispered "don't worry, dear" as he approached Fatima, and walked toward the door. Fatima retreated to her desk, and as she passed to Eric's left she partially obscured his view of Bianca Rodrigues. All that Eric could see of her was her tanned legs, bare to at least the knee. She wore white high-heeled shoes, which were spotted with what Eric presumed to be raindrops. Drops of water fell to the ground alongside her shoes.

Eric walked toward Bianca, and could then make out the tops of her bare thighs. As he approached her, he was grateful to be granted a better view of his visitor. Bianca was sitting with her legs partially crossed and slightly raised, so he could now see what appeared to be a white mini-skirt. The skirt probably came only several inches below her crotch when she was standing, he surmised, and when she was sitting the skirt had ridden up her legs to the point where he could see her pink panties poking out from between her legs. The fabric looked to lessen as it ran down her body, indicating a thong. Eric was pleased with that thought. She again wore a tank top, this time the light green of her native Brazil's flag, and its plunging neckline revealed the hot pink lace bra that, like its predecessor the night before, strained to properly harness its wearer's ample chest. "Bianca," Eric said, "you came back."

Her hair was matted and wet, and drops of rain fell from her hair as she rose to greet him. "So nice to see you again, Mr. Goldberg," she replied as she brushed her hands down her skirt to cover the top of her thighs. "I told you that I would be back. Perhaps you just didn't think it would be so soon." She extended her right hand.

Grasping her hand lightly, Eric said, "No, I didn't. But I am glad that you came back. I assume you have given our conversation some thought…"

"Yes, I have," she interrupted. She looked to the left, where Fatima sat, her head turned toward her computer screen. Looking back to Eric, she lowered her head, and in a soft voice, added, "can we go into your office to talk?"

Eric looked at Fatima, who was now scowling. He smiled at her, looked back at Bianca, and answered, "of course, please." He motioned to his office chair. "You know where to go." She walked toward the leather chair where she had sat the night before, and he followed her through the door. "Looks like you got caught in the rain again today," Eric added, "I hope that it is going to stop soon. It makes everything look so drab and gloomy." Everything, he thought, except for Bianca.

She turned quickly before sitting, beads of water striking Eric in the face as her hair whipped around. "I'm so sorry," she said, raising her hands to her mouth, "I totally forgot to bring your umbrella today. I was rushing to get here and must have left it in my car. I'm so sorry," she repeated, as she wiped water droplets from her left breast, "and I must look like quite the mess." As she wiped the water from her blouse, her wedding ring caught part of the fabric, pulling the tank top down far enough to expose her entire bra-clad breast. "Oh my god," she said while smiling, "I am so embarrassed." She freed her ring from the fabric and pulled green blouse back up over the pink bra. "I don't know what to say," she said as she blushed slightly, "you see how this wedding ring is bad luck for me?"

Bad luck for her, but good luck for him, Eric thought, as he settled down into his own chair, the vision of her lacy pink bra cup emblazoned into his memory. "Very funny," Eric replied, "we'll see what we can do about that bad luck." He motioned to his own shirt. "As for the blouse, don't even give it a second thought," he added, although he knew that he would be thinking about that moment at least a second time, if not many more. He picked up a blue pen from his desk, moved a pad of paper into the center of his desk, and looked at Bianca. "So tell me, what are we doing today?"

Bianca looked down at her blouse, fidgeting with a piece of light green thread which had been pulled from her blouse by her ring. The half-inch long piece of thread stuck out from the blouse slightly above where Eric imagined her nipple would be, and Bianca pulled at it, making it longer. "I need to cut this thread off, Mr. Goldberg. Do you have a pair of scissors?"

"I do," he answered as Bianca continued to paw at the piece of thread like a playful cat. "But you can't cut the thread off while you are wearing the blouse."

With her head still down, she lifted her eyes and peered up at Eric. She asked, coyly, "Mr. Goldberg, do you want me to take it off?" She looked out to where Fatima was sitting and then back at Eric, grabbing the bottom hem of the blouse and slowly lifting it up. "Take it off with the Portuguese girl sitting out there?"

"No, of course not," Eric quickly said, quickly motioning with his hands for her to lower the blouse to its normal position, although he thought of many worse things things that could happen. "Let me explain. It's a Jewish superstition."

"So," asked Bianca, as she let go of the blouse and looked on Eric's desk for scissors, noticing a pair of black-handled scissors standing in a cup with several pens and highlighters. "What does that have to do with me and my blouse?"

"Well," answered Eric, "when someone dies we are supposed to tear our clothes. The superstition is, that if you cut a piece of clothing when you are wearing it, that someone will die."

Bianca eyed him suspiciously. "I have enough of my own things to worry about," she said, as she reached for the scissors. "I can't worry about your Jewish things." She pulled the thread with her left hand and, with the scissors in her right, cut the thread as close to her breast as possible. Placing the scissors alongside some papers that she had piled on the chair next to her, she pulled the sides of the blouse apart with her hands, the fabric stretching tautly over her left breast searching for a possible hole in the fabric. "Do you see a hole in the blouse, Mr. Goldberg? I do not but want to make sure." She stood and leaned over the desk so that Eric could get a better look at the area from where she had cut the offending thread.

Eric gazed into the large breast dangling just inches from his face and gulped. "No," he said quietly, "there are no holes. You did an excellent job of cutting." He paused and took a deep breath as Bianca retreated and again sat down. "Now let's talk about why you are here today."

Bianca fidgeted slightly in the chair, seemingly hesitant to actually say the words that would seal her marriage's fate. She turned her body slightly to the left and uncrossed her legs, again revealing the pink thong that separated her thighs. The fingers of her right hand tapped nervously on the arm of the chair. Seconds of silence passed, and Bianca finally uttered, softly, "I think I want a divorce."

Eric paused, put down the pen, and leaned backward in his chair. "Think?" he said, "or do you know? Because there is a big difference. If you only think that you want to get divorced, then this will be a horrible process for you. You will second-guess yourself constantly." He looked up at her, and the befuddled look on her face belied the fact that she did not understand his last comment. Trying to clarify, he said "You must know for sure. That way, this will be a process that will get you where you want to go, meaning divorced. If you only think that you want it, then every time we talk, every time you see your husband, you will wonder whether you are making the right decision. That's bad for you, and it's a horrible way for me to work." He again paused, and leaned forward in his chair so his chest lay on the desk and Bianca's legs and pink-clad crotch again entered his line of vision. "So I need to know if you are certain, one hundred percent sure, that you want this. Otherwise I don't think it will be a good idea."

Bianca twisted again in her seat, crossing her legs and shifting her body to the right as she looked over Eric's head to the pictures that adorned the wall behind his desk. "Is that your son in the picture with you, Mr. Goldberg?" Bianca asked. She looked closely at the picture, taken when Eric and Jason had attended a Yankees' game the year before. "He is very handsome, just like his father," Bianca said, changing the subject to avoid answering his statement. "Tell me something," she said, now leaning forward so that her nose was a scant few feet from his, "why do you do divorces? Aren't there other types of law that you would rather do than listen to women complain about their husbands all day long?"

Now it was Eric who squirmed in his seat. He exhaled deeply, picked up a pen from his desk and ran it between the fingers on his right hand. He thought for a few seconds, which felt like minutes, and searched the ceiling of his office for the correct response. "You don't really want to know that, do you?" he asked, "I mean," he paused again, "does it really matter?"

"Of course it does, or I wouldn't have asked," whispered Bianca. "Don't you think that your clients want to know things about you? Not just where you went to school, but why you do it, how you are going to fight for us?" She reached out and placed her hand on the edge of his desk, slowly running her fingers across its edge. Her eyes met his. "I already know where you went to school," she said, motioning to the diplomas hanging on the wall behind her. "Now I want to know about you, about why you are the right man for the job."

Eric looked away, out the window to the rain which continued to fall on Broad Street. He wondered what Fatima must be thinking about the conversation between him and Bianca. He wondered if Bianca had seen him watching her as she fidgeted in her seat, how he stared at and underneath the bottom of her skirt as it inched up her thighs. He wondered if he would be able to avoid answering the question, but realized that he would not be able to do so. He again exhaled deeply. "It will sound crazy," he answered.

Bianca's eyes widened. "*Louca?*" she said, "that sounds good to me." She again leaned forward, pressing her breasts together as she folded her arms in front of her. "Tell me something *louca.*"

He glanced down at the breasts again being displayed before him, swallowed, and began to tell Bianca something crazy. "I do it because I want to help people," he began, "well, really, to help kids." He looked for a reaction from Bianca, but none was yet forthcoming. "I do it for the kids." He stopped, waiting for a question of explanation.

The question did not come. Bianca simply uncrossed her arms and leaned back in her chair, nodding her head slowly as if to ask for more.

"My parents were divorced when I was eight," he continued, his eyes misting, "and it was not an easy or amicable one. I found out years later that my mother had cheated on my father, but of course I did not know that when it was happening. I only knew that they were fighting a lot, and that they seemed to hate each other." He paused. "It was horrible."

"It must have been," Bianca said in a comforting voice, "so much for a child to suffer. Do you have any brothers or sisters?"

"I have a sister. She is six years older than me, so she was already 14 when this happened. We had just gotten her Bat Mitzvah album back from the photographers, a book filled with pictures of a happy family, when they told us about the divorce." He rubbed his right eye lightly, moisture covering the outside of his index finger. "So you can imagine it was not easy for me, especially when my father moved out and my mother started saying horrible things about him."

"I was eight. I actually started to believe her. I thought that my dad was somehow the cause of the problems, and tried not to have a good time when he came to get me. It was so unfair of me. I felt totally guilty later when I was older and found out the truth. I apologized to him; he cried and actually apologized to me, even though it wasn't his fault." He wiped another tear from his eye. "It was the first time I ever saw him cry."

"Oh my," Bianca said, as she reached for a tissue from her purse and handed it to Eric. He laughed as he took it from her, and wiped his moistened eyes. "So you think that you can help all of the kids who have families like yours was, is that it?"

"It's never quite that simple," he replied, blowing his nose into a tissue that he retrieved from the box on his desk that was usually reserved for his clients, "but I guess that's one way of putting it. I ruined my relationship with my father for a long time because of what my mother told me. I guess that I became a lawyer to help kids deal with situations like this. I tell the parents to never involve the kids in their problems. I tell them to remind the children how much they love them, and that they are lucky to have two parents who love them even if they live apart."

"And does it work?"

Eric shrugged. "I hope so. At least I hope that it does sometimes. I know that there are people who listen to me, and the kids are much better off with the parents separated than they are dealing with the fighting of unhappy people stuck in a marriage that they hate. On the other hand, I know that there are those who do what my wife, I mean my mother, did when I was a kid. I can't stop them all. But I can try. That's why I do it."

Bianca again looked at the picture of Eric and his son. "You said your wife, you know."

Eric looked at her, puzzled. "What do you mean?"

She smiled faintly. "Just now, you wanted to say that your mother said bad things about your father. But you said your wife, and then corrected yourself." She paused, sensing Eric's discomfort. "Why did you say your wife? Was it just a mistake?"

The pained expression on Eric's face immediately told her the answer. "I meant to say my mother, but whether I said my mother or wife is really no difference. She did the same thing to me. She cheated on me. I know why, because of all of the late hours at work and business dinners. I don't blame her for cheating, sometimes. But she said such horrible things about me to my son that he would barely talk to me for three months leading up to the final divorce hearing." He paused, and again dabbed at his face with the tissue. "Now things are a little better. He splits time between my old house, where the ex-wife still lives, and living with me. But even though things are better with him, they are not like they were before the divorce. They probably never will be the same. And my ex-wife is responsible."

"Just her?" Bianca asked, "or maybe both of you?"

"To be honest," Eric replied, "I can blame her for this one. If she had been mature … if she had listened to the advice that I gave her, like I give to all of my clients, then we all, especially Jason, could have come through the process much better. And amazingly, it looks like we are repeating the same shit that I went through with my father."

"But you didn't think she would listen to you, did you?" Bianca asked. "I know if my husband was telling me how to act during our divorce, I would not listen to him. I would tell him to fuck off and stop telling me what to do."

"That's pretty much what she said to me," Eric said, looking up at the picture. "That's what she said to me. All this time I spend preaching to clients about how to have a good, amicable divorce, and I couldn't even have one myself. But maybe I shouldn't be telling you this, or you will think that I am lousy."

"No," Bianca said firmly, "I think you are a great father, and a person who cares about his clients. I am sure that you will do a good job with my divorce. And I will try to listen to you and not say bad things about their father to my kids." She chuckled lightly. "But it won't be easy."

CHAPTER VI

"I want you to handle the divorce for me, Mr. Goldberg. It won't be easy, but I trust you. He even told me, by the way, that he will fight for custody of the girls. He doesn't want them, he just wants to hurt me," Bianca said as she pulled some of the papers and a manila folder off of the chair. "I brought some of the papers that I thought you would need," she said as she thumbed through the folder's contents, "I have my marriage certificate, birth certificates for the kids, and last year's tax returns. I also have papers from the house, like the last mortgage statement. I am sure there are some other things you will need, but wanted to start today, as soon as possible."

She handed the papers to Eric. He took them and glanced at the tax return, trying to obtain a better idea of her husband's income. The amount owed on the house, as set forth on the latest mortgage statement, seemed pretty high, he reasoned, and there did not appear to be much equity in the house nor did he think that she would be able to keep making the payments on the mortgage without significant help from her husband. But that was all in the future. He had to start the process first, and worry about those details later. "First thing we need to do is take down some information that I will need for the complaint, and have you sign a retainer agreement. That's the agreement between you and I for what you will pay me to represent you."

He swiveled, facing the computer keyboard sitting on his desk, and began to create a retainer agreement for Bianca. "The hourly rate is $300 per hour for the work we do. I think I told you that last night, but don't remember," explained Eric, "and we need $3,500 to begin the work."

Bianca nodded her assent. "OK," she said, "I understand." Eric printed out the retainer agreement, and placed it to his left.

"Now I need some other information to prepare the papers to file with the court," he said. At his request, Bianca provided him with dates of birth for both she and her husband, and for the children. She gave him both of their social security numbers, even though he could have gleaned them from the tax return, and provided him with her driver's license and health insurance cards so that he could make photocopies of each. He took down information about where she was born and the type of car that she drove. When he asked her about various types of insurance, she did not know the names of either their homeowner's or auto insurance companies, but indicated that she would get the information to him later.

The topic of life insurance was, to Eric, interesting. "I don't have any life insurance," Bianca said with a frown, "I guess that he thinks that I am not worth anything." When Eric asked about her husband's life insurance, however, she smiled. "I didn't even know until last night, believe it or not. Last night, after I left here, I went home and went through all of the papers in his desk. He was out late so I had plenty of time to look around after the kids went to sleep." She pulled more pages from her bag. "I found out last night that he has $2 million in life insurance." She laughed. "You know, he's worth much more dead than he is alive. More than I thought, too. Just think how much easier things would be for me," she said, trying to elicit some form of response from Eric. "Think about it," she said again. "I did cut that thread off of my blouse."

"Many people are worth more dead, me included," Eric replied. "Can I see the insurance papers so I can make copies of them? We have to make sure that he doesn't change the beneficiary on the policy before the divorce is finalized. Lots of people try to do that." He took the papers from Bianca. "Are you sure that you are the beneficiary now?"

"Yes. I better be," she said coldly. "After what I have gone through with him and dealing with his bullshit, it's all going to come to me."

Eric started to answer, but paused and looked up from his papers at Bianca. Her smile and easygoing demeanor had vanished. Clearly her emotions were coming to the surface now, her intense dislike for her husband manifesting itself at that moment. "You do realize that he can change the policy once you are divorced; normally people change it to their kids. So then they would at least get the money if something were to happen to him." He could tell that Bianca was still thinking about the problems with her husband in an extreme manner. "And we can make sure that he keeps life insurance for their benefit to guarantee his child support obligations."

Bianca seemed to think for a moment, and her pursed lips separated as her face brightened slightly. "That's after the divorce, right? What about up until the time we are divorced? You said that he can't change anything, right?"

Eric looked at her quizzically, trying to determine her train of thought. "Yes, that's correct," he responded, "until you are divorced he can't legally change the policy. Not that it should matter much. If all goes the way that we want it to, then we will be done with this in about three or four months."

"OK, I thought so. I just wanted to know for sure." She reached for the retainer agreement that rested to Eric's left. "Is this what I have to sign? When do you need money from me?"

Now Eric was puzzled, as Bianca had earlier indicated her understanding that she would have to give him money at the time that she signed the retainer agreement. "Now," he said. "We sign the agreement and you have to give me the check for $3,500." Suddenly, he was thinking about Fatima's words of warning. "Without the money I am not officially retained and do not represent you."

"I'm sorry, Eric," she said, calling him by his first name for the first time while curling locks of her hair with the fingers of her left hand. "I forgot my checkbook." She giggled lightly. "It must be with your umbrella." She glanced downward at her own cleavage. "I'm sometimes surprised that I even remember to get dressed before leaving the house, my memory is so bad. Can you imagine?"

Of course he could. He had been doing so since last night. "I guess so," he said sheepishly. "Tell you what," he added, his voice strengthening as he watched her pull her curls down so they grazed the top of her blouse's neckline, "let's sign the retainer today. I can draft the complaint. When you come back to sign, then you will bring me the check, OK? But remember, until I am paid I am not really retained so it is important that you bring me the check as soon as possible."

"You are so handsome," Bianca answered seductively, "and you are so nice. I am so lucky to have found you." She signed the retainer agreement and handed it back to Eric, her fingers grasping at his as she placed the paper into his hand. "Can I have a copy of this letter? That way I will know how much money I have to bring next time. I promise."

"Of course," Eric responded as he made a copy of the agreement and handed it to her, "but I can't file the complaint until we get paid. It's not that I don't trust you," he added slowly as he gazed into her eyes, "but we have had too much trouble in the past. I have to support myself and Fatima and keep this office running, and I can't do it if I am not getting paid. I am sure you understand." Bianca took the copy from him and shoved it, along with the items from the adjoining chair, into her bag, the insurance policy papers protruding slightly atop the others. She stood, the wrinkled hemline of her skirt remaining perilously close to the bottom of her pink thong. Noticing Eric's quick glance downward, she slowly smoothed the creases of her skirt with her left hand while taking the bag into her right.

"I understand you, Mr. Goldberg, don't worry," she replied, as she again caught his gaze looking downward at her skirt. "I understand you perfectly. I will have your money next time." She turned to leave the office, and walked into the area where Fatima sat, typing and presumably not listening.

Eric followed, three steps behind her, as she strode to the outside door. Bianca turned and smiled at Fatima as she passed her, mouthing the word "*tchau*." Fatima responded with "*obrigada*," Portuguese for thank you, to which Bianca chuckled. Bianca then stopped abruptly, dropped the bag to the floor, and whirled around, standing face-to-face with Eric. She grabbed him in a tight embrace, kissed him on both cheeks, and said, loudly enough for Fatima to hear, "you are a special man, Eric. *Tenho sorte*. I am lucky to have you." Looking over at Fatima, she grabbed Eric closer, her arms clasped tightly on his back and her right cheek pressed against his left.

Stunned, Eric hugged her back, his hands aimlessly running up and down Bianca's back. He experienced an immediate surge of opposing emotions: joy at the feeling of having Bianca's amazing body pressed so tightly against his, but also dread with respect to having to face the proverbial lasers that Fatima was no doubt burning into his body with her cold stare. He couldn't see Fatima; Bianca's head blocked his vision in that direction, but he knew how Fatima would be seething over this display. He knew that Bianca was putting on a show of sorts for Fatima, and that made him feel cheapened. At the same time, however, she was hugging him tightly and the feeling of her body was just as he had imagined. Somehow being cheapened became acceptable.

After what seemed like an eternity, but a blissful eternity, Bianca released her grip on Eric. She pulled slightly backward, again kissing him on both cheeks, and told him that she would be back soon to pay him. She bent down to pick up her bag, the back of her skirt riding up the rear of her thighs and providing Eric with an additional vision of her loveliness, as well as a last peek at the pink strip of fabric running up the crack of her backside. She exaggerated the bend, no doubt for both Eric's and Fatima's benefits, and then stood straight up. As she stood, her right hand clutched the bag, her index finger running up and down the edge of the insurance papers which continued to stick out from the bag's top. The show having ended, Eric turned to retreat into his office, saying "just remember what we have to do. You need to get me money and some more papers."

"Don't worry, Eric," Bianca replied as she looked in Fatima's direction, her fingers continuing to caress the paperwork in her bag while her left hand pushed her hair from her eyes, "I know exactly what I have to do." She stepped closer to the door, reached out with her left hand for the doorknob, and turned before exiting. "I know what I have to do," she repeated. She opened the door, stepped into hallway, and loudly closed the door behind her.

Eric stood in the middle of the office, and nervously looked over at Fatima. He caught her icy stare, and raised both arms at his side and shrugged his shoulders, and asked, quietly, "What do you want me to do?"

"You're kidding me, right?" she bellowed in response, her steely gaze intensifying. "I warned you about her. She's doing exactly what I said she would." Now Fatima sat back and crossed her arms in front of her chest. "Let me guess," she asked, "did she pay you? Did she pay the man who she said is so special and who she is so lucky to have? The man she called 'Eric'?" She brought her right index finger to her open mouth and made a gagging sound after saying his name, as if to emulate someone forcing themselves to vomit.

"Not yet," Eric answered as Fatima's smile grew wider, "but she will. She came back today. She will be back again to pay. Don't worry."

"You're an ass, Eric, you know that?" Fatima replied. "You're a complete ass. She is totally playing you. Just wait, you'll see."

Eric turned to return to his office, wounded by Fatima's lack of self-confidence and seeking to regain some control over the conversation and situation. "You're just jealous," he muttered, immediately regretting saying the words as they came from his mouth.

"Jealous?" Fatima sputtered, "I'm jealous? Are you out of your fucking mind?" Fatima rose from her chair and began muttering in Portuguese, which she often did when angry. She turned away from Eric, then whirled back around and added, "I am anything but jealous, you pompous pig. Fuck you. You deserve her. But don't expect too much. It's all a game to her."

CHAPTER VII

The rain finally ended that evening, just before Eric was set to leave the office. Checking the weather forecast on his computer before shutting it down for the evening, he saw that it called for more rain the next night, which bothered Eric as the next night was Friday, and he was meeting some friends for drinks and to watch the Yankees at a sports bar that had just opened up in nearby Roselle Park. He feared not only that he would be caught in the rain, but, more importantly, that the game might get rained out. He hadn't seen his friends for months now; he had essentially withdrawn from most people while his divorce matter was dragging on, and, even after it was finalized, spent most weekends either with his son, as much as possible, or home alone.

Some of his best friends were married to his ex-wife's best friends, as is so often the case, and the continued relationships between the women made it difficult for some of the men to justify seeing Eric socially. He understood their difficulties. He did not agree with them, but he understood. So the fact that he was able to make plans to meet with three of his friends was, to a certain extent, miraculous and he did not want it ruined by the ridiculous amount of rain that was pelting New Jersey.

The Yankees were returning home from a disastrous West Coast road trip that had left them reeling, dropping several games and falling into third place in the suddenly competitive American

League Eastern Division. That night, the suddenly hot Baltimore Orioles were coming to town to begin a three-game series. If the Yankees could win all three games, they would vault past the birds into second place. On the other hand, if they lost two or three games to the Orioles, there was a distinct possibility that they could fall into fourth place, behind the hated Boston Red Sox. Even though it was only June, therefore, the series was critical to the Yankees' fortunes and eventual chances of making the playoffs. They had to come out strong, and their best pitcher was scheduled to take the mound. A rainout could force him to miss the start, and the Yankees could ill-afford to be forced to play the series without their ace.

Luckily for Eric and the Yankees, the rain that did fall on Friday was minimal. There was enough rain that the Yankee Stadium ground crew spread the tarpaulin on the field during the afternoon as a precautionary measure, but the last drops fell around 5:00. There was, therefore, a two-hour gap between the rain's end and the beginning of the game, so it did not affect the players at all. In Elizabeth and Roselle Park, there were puddles along the streets with which Eric was forced to contend, but he was able to navigate the pathways from his office to the parking lot and then from his eventual parking space in Roselle Park to the sports bar without getting puddle water all over his black shoes or the bottom of his grey suit pant legs.

Game time was 7:05. Eric arrived at the bar at 7:00; Joe and Pete were already waiting for him. As always, Bruce was late. Joe and Pete worked together, and had apparently gone to the bar right from work and had been drinking since 6:30. Already on their second beer, they signaled the bartender to bring one for Eric. The bartender was an attractive woman of Hispanic descent, whom Eric guessed was barely legal age, if even that old. She wore a tight-fitting Yankees Jersey over her black compression shorts, giving the patrons a view of her tanned legs from mid-thigh down to her white sneakers. The jersey was tied into a bunch at the bottom, and Eric could make out the curves of her backside as she turned to retrieve a Michelob for him. When she bent down to take a bottle from the cooler under the bar, all three friends stopped speaking for a second, all six of their eyes transfixed on the beautiful ass being displayed before them.

Bruce showed up about fifteen minutes later, and the foursome decided to remain at the bar to eat. That way they could have immediate access to more drinks, continue to watch the game on the televisions which encircled the bar area, and could continue to watch their new favorite bartender. She said that her name was Luisa, and that she was from Ecuador; by the end of the night, however, none of the four friends remembered either her name or home country, only that she continued to bring their beers upon their command, as well as extra napkins when their nachos and buffalo wings arrived for consumption. Eric and Pete also ate hamburgers and fries, and Bruce inhaled a grilled chicken sandwich along with the appetizers. Joe had to leave early to get home, so he ate only nachos and about a half-dozen wings before leaving in the fourth inning, with the Yankees winning by a 3-1 score.

"Eric," asked Bruce after Joe departed, "We need to talk. I'm a little worried about you. How are things at home?"

"Home?" Eric responded with a question of his own. "You mean the house I can't go to, the apartment I barely tolerate, or the hell-hole of an office where I spend my time with your wife?"

"I mean the apartment," Bruce said, shaking his head. "More to the point, how are things with Jason? Fatima says he doesn't call the office all that often, and we are concerned that you are not seeing enough of him." He paused. "You divorced your wife, you know, you did not divorce your son. In fact, as I am sure you know, he needs you now more than ever."

"I know," Eric replied, now shaking his own head. "He comes and stays with me sometimes, but it's definitely not great. He has school and his friends as diversions from me. I still don't think he has come to grips with the divorce." He chuckled lightly. "It's like the old 'physician, heal thyself' maxim. Let's call it 'attorney, defend thyself.' I spend my days telling clients how to deal with their kids when they separate or get divorced, but I am clearly incapable of properly handling my own son."

"It will get better," Pete chimed in. "He's a good kid. He just needs to sort things out. Maybe have him come along the next time we get together, and if he sees you with us, not just as a dad or as the guy that divorced his mother, it will humanize you a little more."

"That's a great idea," Bruce added. "Besides, it would be nice to get to see him. It's not like he's in college halfway across the country."

"I can try," Eric said as the next Yankee stepped up to bat. "But I can't make any promises. He's stubborn, like his mother."

The game ended at 11:15, a quick game by Yankee standards, and with the home team emerging victorious by a decisive 5-1 count. Eric and his friends remained at the bar for another hour, talking about the game, the Yankees, and reminiscing. By the time he left, the final tally for Eric showed four beers, enough nachos and chicken wings to last him for a week, a hamburger, a plate full of fries, and the thrill of seeing his friends and being sociable again. He arrived home to a dark apartment a little after 12:30; the only sounds he could hear were the dueling snores of his son and dog as they slept in Jason's room. He wearily climbed into bed, thoughts of the evening competing in his mind with visions of Bianca Rodrigues.

CHAPTER VIII

Saturday was the first bright sunny morning in recent memory, and the sunlight peeking through her bedroom's blinds awoke Fatima. Lifting her head up off of her pillow, she could see the outline of her husband's back underneath the blanket next to her and could hear from his heavy breathing that he was still asleep. Looking to the clock on the cable box situated beneath the television in her bedroom, she could see that the time was 7:42. Saturday was the one day of the week that she could sleep late, so she had no desire to leave the comfort of her bed, but, realizing that she was awake and fearful of waking her husband if she remained in the bed, she decided that she would go downstairs, make herself a cup of coffee, and read the newspaper.

Reaching to the edge of the bed, she found her pink robe and wrapped it around her body. Silently tip-toeing to the bedroom door, she quietly opened it and left it slightly ajar so as not to make noise while closing it. She walked down the carpeted steps carefully, trying to avoid the sections of the steps which creaked when being traversed. Reaching the kitchen, she poured water into the percolator, added several scoops of coffee grinds to the upper steel basket, and plugged the machine into the wall. Waiting until she heard the familiar sounds of bubbling water to confirm that the coffee was being properly made, she leaned against the island located in the center of her kitchen and gathered up the remains of the previous day's newspaper to throw into the recycling bin located outside of her side door.

Walking to the side door, Fatima opened the door and stepped out into the warm sunlight. Tossing the old newspaper into the bin which sat alongside the house she walked, barefoot, down the driveway. Reaching down, she retrieved that morning's paper. Folded in half and secured by an elastic band, half of the banner headline, decrying the legislature's latest moves regarding public pensions, leapt off the page. Standing, she saw her neighbor running up the street. She waved to the man as he passed, tucked the paper under her right armpit, inhaled the sweet air of placid suburbia, and walked back into her kitchen.

The smell of freshly-brewed coffee wafted through the sunlit kitchen, mixing with the lingering smells from outside in Fatima's nose. Fatima walked into the kitchen, inhaled deeply, and reached for a coffee mug from the cupboard. She took a carton of milk from the refrigerator, a tub of sugar from the cupboard, and poured coffee, milk, and two teaspoons of sugar into the mug. Stirring the coffee with a teaspoon, she reached for the newspaper, gently placed the spoon into the kitchen sink, and walked to the kitchen table, newspaper in one hand and her coffee in the other.

The first section of the newspaper was fairly standard news fodder. Articles recounted trouble in Trenton with the legislature, some type of storm in Japan, and rising tensions in the Middle

East. Nothing held Fatima's attention. The second section, the Union County section, contained an article on local schools which seemed interesting. After six paragraphs, the article continued on the next page. Sipping her coffee as she turned the page, her eyes opened wide and she almost spit the coffee into the air when she saw the headline on page 15.

CHAPTER IX

"A lawyer shall not counsel or assist a client in conduct that the lawyer knows is illegal, criminal, or fraudulent …"

- New Jersey Rules of Professional Conduct Paragraph 1.2(d)

The ringing of the phone reverberated through the apartment as light gleamed through its window blinds. Eric's head was buried in his pillow, but he could hear the sounds of Jason walking slowly in the kitchen and Jason's muffled voice answering the phone. The sound of Jason's steps grew louder, and were followed by a knock on the bedroom door. "Dad," Jason called out, "Fatima is on the phone. She says it is important." Jason opened the door, walked into the room, and again repeated to his semi-conscious father, "Fatima's on the phone. She says it is important."

Eric raised his head from the pillow, his grogginess making the head feel like it weighted a ton. The clock on his nightstand read 8:15. His head throbbed from the previous night's beers. "I'll tell you, Jason, your old man can't go out anymore. I only had a couple of beers and feel like shit." He looked up, squinting into the light, and tried to focus on his son's face. "You said it was Fatima calling me this early? She didn't wake you up, did she?"

Jason's right hand was cupped over the phone's mouthpiece, and he attempted to stifle a yawn with his left hand.

"No, don't worry. I've got some work to do for school anyway. But she sounds really upset, Dad. You'd better talk to her."

"Sure, just hand me the phone," Eric mumbled, pawing at his reddened eyes with his left hand while he reached for the phone with his right. "Is it really only 8:15?"

"Yes it is, Dad. Here's the phone." Jason handed Eric the phone and then turned to leave the room.

"Jason?" Eric said, "maybe we can do something today."

"Don't think so dad," Jason replied. "You wanted me to take this summer class. I've got to do some work for a presentation next week, so I am going to Adam's. We are going to work on it together and then we are going to hang out, and probably go to the movies later with some of the other guys."

Eric looked at him with a pained look on his face, a look which also belied the fact that he knew that Jason was simply avoiding spending time with him. "If you say so," Eric said, sadly. "But if your plans happen to fall through, let me know. I have no plans for tonight, so we can spend some time together. We can go to the movies if you want, my treat, of course."

"Sure thing, dad, I will keep you posted," Jason said, closing the door behind him as Peyton trotted at his side. Eric knew, however, that he was not being sincere and that, no matter what happened to the rest of Jason's day, his son's plans would not include him.

As Jason closed the door, Eric sat up in his bed, leaning back against his pillow as he pulled the phone to his face. "What's up, Fatima? Why are you calling me at this insane hour? You know I was out with the guys last night."

"Did you see today's newspaper?" Fatima demanded excitedly, without responding to Eric's questions. "Did you see the paper yet?"

"Calm down, Fatima. No, I have not seen the paper. The phone woke me up." He coughed, the throbbing in his temples intensifying. "I'm a bit hung over. What's in the paper that is so important?"

"He's dead," she shrieked. "It's in the second section of the paper."

Holding the phone from his ear to avoid making his headache worse, Eric struggled to digest what Fatima was saying. "Wait, wait. Someone's dead? Who's dead?"

Before he could complete the second question, Fatima was already answering. "Joao Rodrigues. That's who. Joao Rodrigues is dead."

"John Rodrigues?" he answered, his lack of a Portuguese accent Americanizing the man's name. "Is that who I think it is?"

"Damn fucking right it is!" she answered, "Bianca's husband. He's dead."

Now the cobwebs were leaving Eric's mind, and the throbbing of his temples was secondary to his feelings of concern. "Shit," he replied, "how?"

"He had a car accident, according to the article. He ran right into a pole on Ferry Street last night." She paused, and then said, in a lower voice, presumably so her husband would not hear her, "the article says that police are investigating, Eric. They think it's suspicious. Do you think she could have done it?"

Eric struggled to retain his composure. "Honestly, no, I don't." He leapt out of bed. "Let me take a look at the paper and we will talk later. But don't tell anyone that she was in to see us. You haven't told Bruce that she was in the office, have you?"

"No," she answered. "I didn't tell him, and haven't told anyone from my family either." She sighed. "That would have been far worse than telling Bruce, because you know how that shit gets around the old neighborhood." She paused, and Eric could hear her rapid, hyperventilating-type breaths through the phone. "I told you that she was trouble. What the fuck have you gotten us into?"

"Nothing," he said, feigning calm, "just relax." Now Eric's heart was racing also, and his voice growing more excited. "Let me check out the paper. Relax and I will call you later."

"Okay, I will try to relax." She laughed nervously. "Is it too early to have a drink?"

"Never. It's never too early," he answered. "I will call you later." He clicked the phone off, threw on a shirt, and ran out to the kitchen. "Jason," he called, "where is today's newspaper?"

From his own bedroom, Jason called out to his father. "I didn't bring it in yet, dad. It's probably still out in the hallway." By that time Eric was already at the front door. Turning the deadbolt lock, he thrust the door open and bent down to pick up the newspaper sitting on the welcome mat, groaning as he stood back up with that day's copy of *The Star Ledger* in his possession. Returning to the kitchen, he tore the rubber band off of the folded newspaper and frantically turned the pages, searching for the article about the dead Portuguese construction manager.

His search was a short one. On Page 15, the headline practically leapt out at him: "*Local business owner dies in car crash.*" The article confirmed what Fatima had told him a few minutes before, that Joao Rodrigues' car had crashed into a pole on Ferry Street in Newark's Ironbound section, a scant few blocks from a house that he was in the process of rehabilitating for sale. The article also stated that the police were deeming the cause of accident as "suspicious," and that, according to the police, the rains from the previous days had not played a role in the crash as that section of Ferry Street had not been wet at the time of the accident. The article concluded with the following:

Rodrigues leaves behind a legacy of renovated properties throughout his home city of Newark and Union County. He leaves behind his wife of ten years, Bianca, and his two daughters, Carla, age ten, and Leila, age five. Funeral arrangements are pending. In lieu of flowers, it is requested that donations be made to a scholarship fund that has been established for the girls' benefit.

Carla. Leila. Somehow, seeing the daughter's names in print made Eric queasy. He couldn't understand why. All of the divorce complaints that he had filed over the years included children's names and dates of birth, why was this any different? Perhaps it was the finality of it all. At least when people got divorced the children still had both of their parents. As he had explained to the newly-widowed Bianca Rodrigues only two days earlier, he tried his best to make certain that children of divorce maintained strong relationships with both parents.

That could not be the case with Carla and Leila Rodrigues. Their father was gone. They would never have a relationship with him. And that bothered Eric greatly.

His thoughts shifted to Bianca. Had she said anything that indicated that she was capable of doing this? Could she possibly have been that upset with him? Certainly she was mad, but to somehow cause a car accident that would deprive her daughters of their father? No, that did not seem possible. She would be at the funeral consoling her daughters. No woman could want that for her children. They would lean on her for support, at the funeral and thereafter. The funeral. That would be difficult, he thought. Everyone would be crying. Everyone would be wearing black. "I wonder what Bianca would look like in a little black dress?" he wondered aloud.

"What, Dad?" Jason called from the adjoining room.

Eric had not realized that he had verbalized that last question. "Oh, nothing, Jason. I was just talking to myself," he answered, "nothing for you to worry about." Now Eric made sure to keep his thoughts silent. What would she wear? Would she wear a little black dress? Probably with some lace, no doubt, and ending above the knee. She would probably have a lacy black bra underneath. No stockings in this heat, so her legs would be exposed down to her black heels. He wondered if she would cross and uncross her legs during the funeral service like she had while in his office. Or would the dress be short enough so that it would ride up her legs while she dabbed at her eyes with tissues? Would the priest be able to see her thong, no doubt a black one, as she sat in the front row of the service for her own husband's funeral?

He caught himself, realizing that this line of thought was improper. The woman's husband had just died. It was wrong of him to think of her in a sexual way at the funeral. Or was it? He wouldn't be at the funeral, so it was all just wishful thinking. So he sat there, in his kitchen, becoming aroused at the idea of the woman who would no longer need his services for a divorce from her now-deceased husband.

He read the article again. And then he read it for a third time.

According to police, preliminary investigation revealed that the vehicle may have been tampered with. Police also indicated that the recent wet weather did not play a role in the accident, and that they were also discounting the possibility of human error. Although the van was badly burned in the accident, police were able to recover various items from the vehicle which they hope will reveal more clues to its cause.

Tampered? Is it possible that Bianca could have done something to the van to cause the accident? Why would she come in to his office one day, and then kill her husband the next? It just didn't make sense to Eric. Did Eric say anything to her that would have caused her to change her plan to divorce him?

And what if he did think that she had done something? What would he do? What could he do? She was his client. Even though she hadn't paid him yet, he believed, she would still be considered to be his client. Anything that they had discussed was privileged, and he could not tell anyone else about their conversations, including the police. He struggled to think back to law school – he recalled that if someone said that they were going to kill someone, then the attorney could tell the authorities. But she had never given any indication that she was thinking of murdering her husband, did she? No, she had not. They did make a joke about his life insurance, he remembered, but that was it. So there was no way he could go to the police.

Should he call her? See if she was somehow involved, or even just to express his condolences? He could tell her to go to the police and turn herself in if she had played a role in the crash – but, then again, would she even listen to him? He poured himself a cup of coffee and sat at the kitchen table, burying his head in his hands. He was unable to properly formulate his thoughts. He had to talk to someone. He was reaching for the phone to call Fatima when he was surprised by a voice.

"Hey dad, what's the problem?" Eric heard Jason ask. "You look worried about something. Anything I can do to help?"

The question surprised Eric, because this was the first time that Jason had expressed any interest in his life, or his concerns, for as long as he could remember. Even though his son was reaching out to him, however, this was a topic that he could not share with him. "Nothing's up, Jason," replied Eric, "I'm just reading the paper and haven't had my coffee yet." He held his cup, still full of hot coffee, aloft as proof. "But thanks for asking. I really do appreciate it."

Jason walked closer and peered over his father's shoulder. He looked down at the newspaper on the table and stepped back. "Obituaries, huh?" he asked, "no wonder you look depressed. Who wants to read about dead people?"

CHAPTER X

"A lawyer shall reveal [information relating to the representation of a client] to the proper authorities, as soon as, and to the extent the lawyer reasonably believes necessary, to prevent the client or another person ... from committing a criminal, illegal or fraudulent act that the lawyer reasonably believes is likely to result in death or substantial bodily harm ..."

- New Jersey Rules of Professional Conduct Paragraph 1.6

Justin Green sat at his desk, alternately looking out the picture window that wrapped around the corner of his office and at his computer monitor, which showed his beloved Philadelphia Phillies being routed by the Washington Nationals – it was the sixth inning of a Wednesday matinee game, and the Phils' bats were being stymied by the Nationals' pitchers. The Philadelphia starting pitcher had not fared so well, and sat on the short end of a 4-0 score. The home team was careening toward its fifth straight loss, and with this defeat would settle into the basement of the National League East, a division whose top spot was occupied by Washington.

Outside the window, traffic crawled along Route 70. The various office parks around Cherry Hill had just undergone the daily ritual of the 5:00 worker and vehicle exodus, and Justin smirked with the knowledge that he would be in the office for at least another couple of hours, thereby avoiding all of the traffic.

Justin Green's office walls were decorated with various awards, including a plaque which recognized him as the Camden County winner of the Ethics award for 2010. To its left was a plaque which recognized Green's service as the chair of the county's Ethics panel from 2007 through 2009, and below that plaque was a framed picture of Green with his two sons and the two New Jersey senators that was taken in Washington, DC during a recent family trip.

One other picture was hung in the office – a picture of Green taken at his law school graduation with four of his best friends – Pete Harper, John Harvey, Eric Goldberg and Jonathan Grant.

He glanced at the computer screen, which now showed the deficit being cut in half, to 4-2, after a two-run homer by one of the Phillies' reserve outfielders. The cell phone on his desk hummed – looking down, he saw the word "Eric" on the screen.

Reaching down, he picked up the phone and pushed the "answer" button. "Goldie!" he barked into the phone. "To what do I owe the pleasure of this call?"

"Thought I would get you on the cell," answered Eric Goldberg's voice, "you still in the office?"

"Of course, fool. What do you think, I'm working half-days now? I'm here until at least seven." He paused. "Plus, you wouldn't catch me dead in that traffic. And I am watching the Phils go down again. I hate these matinee games. They just get me depressed earlier in the day when the Phillies lose. How are things up North?"

"The usual," answered Eric, "working like a dog, making my few cents, dodging a few bullets. And of course the Phillies are losing. What do you expect from those guys? They aren't good, you know."

"I hope you didn't call just to insult my team, dude. Some of us have real work to do."

"No, that's not why I called." Eric replied, his voice growing somber. "I need some advice."

Justin leaned back in his chair. "Really," he said, "what's up?"

Eric sighed audibly through the phone, catching Justin by surprise. After a long pause, he began to speak. "It's an ethics question. You're the guru on ethics in this state," he said, again pausing before adding, "I need to know what you think about a situation."

"Seriously?" Justin asked, "this sounds heavy. Tell me and I will see if I can give you a hand."

"Here goes," replied Eric, "what would you do if you think that a client of yours did something wrong … no, make that really, really wrong."

"That is first-year law school stuff, Eric, you know that. A little thing we learned called the attorney-client privilege. You sat behind me in class, so I know that you heard it. You can't say anything. Surely you know that …"

Eric interrupted his friend – "no, Justin, I mean really, really wrong. Criminally wrong. Seriously wrong."

"It doesn't matter. Anything a client tells you that he did is privileged. You can't tell anyone. I've had to sanction people down here for breaking the privilege. It can't be done."

Eric sighed again. "Let me try this again. What if it is something that your client did, not something that she said to you?"

Justin laughed. "I should have known it would be a she. Guess that changes things. You want to tell me what this female client of yours allegedly did? Or, better yet, tell me what she looks like?"

"She's really hot, to be honest with you, but that is completely off-topic," said Eric, hearing Justin's continued laughter through the phone. "Please listen to me. I am really calling you for advice."

Justin cleared his throat. "Sorry. I couldn't resist. You know my wife would kill me if she heard me talking like that. What's bothering you?"

"What if one of your clients," he paused before repeating himself, "what if one of your clients, say, killed someone? She didn't tell you, but you just know. Then what do you do?"

"Are you saying that one of your clients killed someone?"

"I think so."

"Well, that's pretty weird. But …"

"What?"

"The answer is still the same. You can't say anything. The only way that you could is if she told you that she was going to kill or hurt somebody specific and you thought that she would do it. Then, to protect the person you would be justified in telling the police. But if the deed is done, so to speak, then you have to keep it to yourself."

"Here's another twist for you, then. What if she signed a retainer agreement, but still has not paid the retainer fee. Is she still technically a client?"

"The the attorney is either an idiot," Justin replied, "or figured that he would be paid in a different form later. Either way, though, you can't say anything. Once you have spoken to her and signed an agreement, even if she didn't pay your stupid ass, you can't say anything to anybody."

Eric breathed deeply. "How did I know you were going to say that?"

"Because," Justin answered, "you really aren't a stupid ass, and you called me to confirm what you already knew. The real advice that I will give you is to avoid this person, if you really think that she was capable of doing it. But don't jump to conclusions unless you are certain. It is unfair of you to condemn her if she did not do anything wrong."

"I know, I know," Eric murmured.

"Especially if she is hot," Justin added.

"You're an asshole. Go home and give your wife a kiss for me."

"Alright, man, talk to you soon." Justin said, as he hung up the phone, wiped his eyes, and cursed the professional responsibility rules and his rigid adherence to following them.

CHAPTER XI

The streets of São Paulo, as always, were cluttered with cars, stretching from one end of the horizon, it seemed, to the other. The third-largest city in the world, located in the southern part of Brazil, is home to ten million people; on this day, it also appeared to contain 20 million cars. In the middle of this traffic, spending what seemed like his third hour on Paulista Avenue, watching the pedestrians walk past the *Museu de Arte de São Paulo*, sat Steve Cooper. "I can't believe this shit," he muttered to himself, "three years in this damned city and I still can't figure out the traffic patterns. I just want to get the hell home."

Home, to Steve Cooper, was Mooca, a neighborhood on the other side of São Paolo that possessed a strong Italian influence, an influence which reminded him of his upbringing in New York City, where he was born 24 years earlier. He had left the city to major in architecture at Penn State University; during his junior year he decided to study abroad and settled on spending the spring semester in São Paulo, where he clerked with Edson Marques Arquitetos, one of Brazil's largest architecture firms, working in its main office in the center of the city. He became fascinated with the city's architecture, stayed through the summer, and decided to settle in São Paulo following his graduation, to work in the city for a few years before returning, most likely, to live in the United States.

Living in Mooca afforded him the best of both worlds, he reasoned. It allowed him to live in São Paulo and experience Brazil, while at the same time allowing him to feel comfortable in a neighborhood that, to him, most resembled the United States and his home.

"*Eu deveria ter estudado matemática ou engenharia* (Should have studied math or engineering)," he said to himself, in broken Portuguese, as the air choked with the exhaust from thousands of vehicles. "Then", he added in slightly-accented English, "I could have really served a purpose down here. I could be the guy who solved the traffic problems." He looked at the dozens of cars within his vicinity, most of which were occupied with guys like him, men who had worked a full day and were now just struggling to return to their homes and families. "There's got to be a better way."

Over an hour later, he arrived home – climbing the steps to his second-floor apartment, he could hear muted bossa nova music and the smell of dinner emanating from behind the apartment door. Opening the door, he could see into the kitchen; a pot of boiling water sat atop the stove, with curls of white smoke rising lazily into the air. The smell of fried chicken filled his nostrils, and the half-full bag of white rice sitting alongside the pot of boiling water signaled another dinner of chicken and rice, the preferred meal of his girlfriend, Leticia Alves.

22 years old and native-born Brazilian, Leticia stood a statuesque 5 feet, 10 inches tall and, with her flattened stomach, 24-inch waist and C-cup breasts, was often mistaken for a model. Captivated immediately upon meeting the six foot-two American who worked with her father at the architectural firm, she had moved most of her belongings into his apartment three months earlier and, while acting as a substitute teacher and looking for a full-time job after graduating from *Universidade de São Paulo*, had spent her time mastering her cooking skills for her (in her mind) possible future husband.

"*Frango e arroz novamente?* (Chicken and rice again?)" he asked upon seeing Leticia, clad only in a t-shirt and tiny white shorts, "it's the third time this week we've had chicken and rice."

"*O seu Português está ficando muito melhor, meu amor*", she purred in response, repeating in English so that he definitely understood – "your Portuguese is getting much better, my love." Though born and raised in São Paulo, Leticia had spent several years in the United States, living in Miami, when her father had been working with a firm in Florida and spoke fluent English in addition to her native tongue.

"*Obrigado*", he replied, thanking her for the compliment as he bowed slightly, "*Eu tentando. Mas, não é fácil.* (I am trying, but it is not easy)."

"Apparently it is not. You should have said '*Eu estou tentando, meu amor*,'" she cautioned, moving toward Steve and wrapping her arms around his waist. Pulling him tightly against her ample chest, she added, "without the '*estou*', you said 'I trying', not 'I am trying'."

"I could always try harder," he said, as he lowered his head to kiss her neck, which shone brightly in the sun filtering through the apartment window, Leticia's hair pulled back tightly into a ponytail. "*Mas, não é fácil.*"

"It is easy if you practice," she replied, arching her back and moving her head backward to expose more of her neck to her lover's kisses. Her hands ran up and down his back, eventually settling into the back of his pants' waistband. "Try this: *devo mover minhas mãos, ou deixá-los onde eles estão?* (shall I move my hands, or leave them where they are?)" She pulled her neck away from his lips, and looked into his eyes for a response.

Steve thought about the question for a moment, clearly distracted by Leticia's fingernails tapping against the small of his back. "Ask me again, please," he stated, trying to focus on the individual words. He understood that "*mover minhas mãos*" meant "move my hands" but wanted to make sure that he gave the right answer – did she want to move her hands, or leave them where they were? If she moved them, did she mean downward or out of his pants?

"OK," she whispered, bringing her head closer to his, so that her mouth hovered a scant few inches from his right ear. "*Devo mover minhas mãos, ou deixá-los onde eles estão?*"

As her hot breath entered his ear, he tried desperately to determine the right answer. "*eles estão*" must mean "them here", he reasoned. He decided to be clever, and ask her to move them down even lower. "*Não, movê-las para baixo,*" he answered.

She moved her head even closer to his ear, so that he could feel her upper lip resting against the top of his ear. "Really?" she cooed, "*movê-las para baixo?* Move them down?" She gently kissed his ear, and started to move her hands downward into the back of his pants before pulling them out and stepping away from him. "*Desculpe, meu amor,* (I am sorry, my love,)" she said, pulling at her t-shirt to better show off her breasts, "*estou preparando o jantar. Eu não tenho tempo para brincar.*" She turned and sashayed to the kitchen, her hips swaying in an exaggerated manner as she walked.

He understood that completely. Tucking his shirt back into his pants, he followed her into the kitchen, protesting, "if you had to cook dinner and had no time for play, then why did you even start with me?"

She turned, her ponytail whipping to the right before settling onto her shoulder. "*Porque eu posso,*" she replied, licking her lips for added effect, "*porque eu posso. Me entendes?*"

Steve shook his head sadly. "I understand you. You said because you can, right?"

"Yes, *meu amor*," Leticia responded as she began to prepare dinner, again swiveling her hips in an exaggerated motion. Steve sighed. They both knew that she was completely correct.

CHAPTER XII

Eric paced nervously around his office. It was 8:55 am on Monday morning. He had not slept well, or even for his normal amount of less-than-necessary hours, for an entire week, and his reddened eyes darted furiously from wall to wall as he awaited Fatima's arrival. The weekend, and two days away from the office, had done nothing to lessen his nervousness about the death of Joao Rodrigues. He wanted to believe that Bianca had not done anything to contribute to her husband's death, but he was certain that, somehow, she had been responsible for the vehicle's failure.

He felt paralyzed by the fact that he could do nothing about it. One of the first things that he had learned in law school was the attorney-client privilege, the same code of silence that was drilled into his head again the prior week by his friend Justin and the same concept which he had heard time and time again in movies and television, and even in casual conversation, since he was a young boy. It was an oath that he took quite seriously – he often wondered if his lack of candor with his wife about the events of workdays had contributed to his divorce, but he believed that his client's secrets, especially those of his divorce and criminal clients, where any information that he possessed was likely embarrassing and could not be repeated, were sacred. Almost ridiculously, this was true even where, as here, she had not even paid him a dime yet for his efforts and aggravation.

This was the first time that he truly wanted to tell someone, and what he wanted to tell was not even something that a client had told him in confidence. Bianca never told him that she had even thought of hurting, much less killing, her husband. Yes, she had said that "I know what I have to do," but that could have meant anything. It could have meant move out of the house with her children. It could have meant cleaning out all of the bank accounts to ensure that he could not take the money. It could have meant that she would have an affair to get even with him, and it could even have meant that she would have considered having that affair with Eric. And she did joke about having cut the thread off of her blouse, but that certainly was not sufficient to prove to anyone that she had threatened to murder her husband.

She also did have access to his van, he knew, because he remembered her telling him that she was driving that vehicle on the night of their first consultation. Still, it was not unlikely that a person would be driving their spouse's car, and the mere fact that she had the vehicle could not lead to the assumption that she somehow tampered with it and caused the accident that led to his death.

He stopped pacing and looked to the chair where Bianca had been sitting during their first meeting, where he first gazed upon her beautiful face, flowing hair, and flawless body. His eyes widened. "Shit," he said aloud, "we also discussed his insurance policies. What did she say he had, a couple of million dollars in insurance? And me laughing at her stupid, and way too obvious, joke about him being worth more dead than alive? What if I put the idea into her head? Oh, fuck." His mind was whirring a mile a minute, and he knew that all of his hypotheses were just that – theoretical. He had no real proof, of any kind, that the accident was not just that, an accident.

That the police were not convinced, at least publically, could have been mere lip service. Perhaps the police really did not think that it was anything but an unfortunate accident, and were merely making public pronouncements of an investigation in order to protect themselves from any second-guessing. Besides, a week had gone by with no further updates from the police as to whether or not they had any further information on the accident or as to whether they were going to charge anyone, including Bianca, with any wrongdoing. There was no buzz on the streets of Elizabeth or Newark, notably, which could have convinced Eric that he was obsessing over nothing.

Yet he was still concerned, still not sleeping, and still pacing in his office. In a way, he did not even know why. There was nothing that he could have done to prevent a murder if he did not know of the perpetrator's intent, and he was now bound by his code of ethics from even telling anyone if he suspected or had any real evidence to suggest that Bianca was culpable in any way. It made no logical sense. His brain knew that. But his gut told him something else.

He looked at his watch. 9:02. Where the hell was Fatima? Damned Monday traffic.

CHAPTER XIII

"The lawyer owes entire devotion to the interest of the client, warm zeal in the maintenance and defense of his rights and the exertion of his utmost learning and ability, to the end that nothing be taken or be withheld from him…"

- American Bar Association Canons
of Professional Ethics Paragraph 15

The outer office door flew open, startling Eric as the heavy wood frame of the door rattled on its hinges after striking the adjacent wall. Eric, hearing the indiscernible muttering of a woman who had just braved Monday morning traffic to get to work, turned and walked outside of his room, saying "Jesus, Fatima, where have you …" Looking up, he stopped in his tracks. Fatima was not in the office. There, standing ten feet away from Eric, was Bianca Rodrigues.

But she was a different Bianca Rodrigues. Her long, flowing hair was pulled back tightly in a ponytail, and she wore no makeup. Her eyes were reddened and swollen, likely from crying, and her nail polish was chipped and clearly had not been touched up for days. For clothing, she wore muted colors, although her brown blouse was still cut low enough down her chest to allow Eric to catch a glimpse of the leopard-print bra that she had worn to the office before.

"Bianca," he stammered, "what … what are you doing here?"

She looked to the floor. "I had to come see you. Sorry I did not call first." She looked back up at Eric, her eyes moistened. "My husband … my husband," a tear fell from her left eye, "my husband died."

"I know," he replied, "I read about it in the papers. I did not think it would be right to bother you about it last week."

She looked into his eyes, and a slight smile formed across her lips. "That's so nice of you," she said, "I was right. You are a nice man."

"Do you want to come in and talk?"

"Yes," she said, walking toward him. She put her arms around his shoulders and drew him in to a forceful embrace. "I do need to talk to you."

Eric felt her chest pressing against his. He also felt the front of his pants beginning to strain, and pulled away from her and turned to walk back into his office, behind his desk, and quickly sat down to hide the evidence of his impure thoughts. Bianca followed him into the room and sat in the chair across from his desk. She lifted her left hand to wipe the tear from her cheek, and the bottom of her blouse lifted to reveal the top of her thong peeking above the top of her pants. The straining in Eric's pants increased.

"So you know how my husband died, then?" she asked.

Eric shifted in his seat. "Yes, I heard it was a car accident."

"The police came and talked to me." She paused, looking out the window. "Someone over there seems to think that it wasn't a real accident." She looked back to Eric. "They think that someone did something to the car. But I didn't do it."

Eric gazed back at her, directly into her reddened eyes. "Of course not," he answered. "Have they told you anything else? I know there has been nothing in the papers."

She sighed. "I am so glad I came here. I need to talk about this but can't talk to anyone. But you're my lawyer, right? So I can talk to you about anything?"

"Yes," he said, "the old attorney-client privilege. Whatever you say here …" he saw her smile seem to increase in size, "stays here, even though you still haven't paid me yet." He winced as the words exited his mouth, realizing that his comment was in bad taste considering the current circumstances, and thought it best to move on without belaboring that obviously tacky detail. "What did you want to …"

He was interrupted by the ringing of his cell phone. Glancing down to the phone resting on his desk, he could see Fatima's picture on the screen. "Sorry, it's my secretary."

"The Portuguese girl?" she said, somewhat defiantly, "you better answer."

"Of course I will. But be quiet," he said, holding his finger up to his mouth in a "silence" pose. Eric picked up the phone and punched in the access code. "Hello?"

Even Bianca could hear Fatima's voice through the phone. "I don't think I will be able to come in this morning, Eric," she yelled. "We were up all last night with some kind of stomach thing. I feel like shit. I need to sleep."

He looked nervously at Bianca. "OK, no problem." He said. "The calendar is clear today anyway so you stay home and rest." He looked away from Bianca. "I will see you …"

This time his sentence was interrupted by a crash in his office. Bianca, squirming in her seat, and leaning too close to the desk, had inadvertently knocked one of the files off of the desk, which hit the ground with a resounding thud.

Fatima heard the sound through the phone. "Is someone there with you?" she asked.

Eric paused. "No," he answered, not wanting to draw any ire or judgmental diatribe from his assistant, "I am here alone. I knocked the Heath file off of my desk by accident. Or maybe it was subconsciously on purpose. You know what a pain in the ass he has been."

"Oh, OK," she replied. "I may try to make it in this afternoon if your cousin can come home and watch the kids. If not, then I will see you tomorrow morning." He could hear muffled sounds, as if children were whining in the background, and silently thanked God that he no longer had small children. "Thanks for understanding."

"Any time, my dear," he answered. "Any time. Get some sleep and I will see you tomorrow." He clicked off the phone and placed it back down on his desk, and now saw that Bianca's smile had, in fact, grown broader.

"So the Portuguese girl isn't coming in today?" she asked.

"Nope," Eric answered, "home sick with the kids."

"I know that feeling," Bianca answered. "When I was working, I had to stay home sometimes when kids were sick. I was lucky to have a good boss." Her voice lowered. "The Portuguese girl is lucky to have a good boss. Do you think that she knows how lucky she is?" Again bringing her left hand to her cheek while she looked out the door at the rest of the office, she asked, "do you have any tissues?"

Eric stared for a minute at the empty tissue box on his desk. "I used to," he replied, "but it seems that I am all out," he added, picking up the empty box and running his fingers through its top opening to confirm that it was devoid of any additional tissues.

"Fatima has some on her desk." He began to stand, cautiously, "let me get you some."

She waved her hand. "No," she ordered, "you sit. I will get them." He gratefully sat as she stood. As she bent to push her hands down on the arms of the chair, the top of her blouse fell down her left shoulder, exposing her bra strap and a good portion of her bra-encased left breast. She did nothing to fix it as she stood and walked out to Fatima's desk.

Eric could feel the strain on the front of his pants increasing. He could hear the Bianca pulling several tissues from the box on Fatima's desk, and then heard what he thought was the sound of the front door locking.

Bianca walked back into his office. Her blouse still hung limply on her left arm, her bra exposed, as she dabbed at her eyes with a tissue held in her right hand. She gazed at Eric, squirming uncomfortably in his seat. "I need your help, Mr. Goldberg," she said. "I need your help with the police. I didn't do anything. I need for them to know that."

He could not help but notice the irony in the fact that she called him "Mr. Goldberg" rather than by his first name, especially as she was clearly and proudly displaying her breast to him.

She walked to the side of his desk, her left hand slowly running its fingers along the edge. Her blouse fell even more as she walked, and now her entire breast was free of its fabric. "Will you help me?" she asked, breathlessly, "Will you?"

"Of ... of course I will," Eric stammered as she drew closer. "What do you want me to do? Call the police and speak to them about something?"

"Maybe," she replied. She was now standing right next to him. His chair was still facing forward, his legs under the desk. He avoided turning the chair toward her so that she would not see his arousal. "Turn to me," she said, "*olhe para mim.* How's your Portuguese? Look at me."

He glanced to his left to see her lifting her blouse up over her head. She tossed the blouse to the chair where she had been sitting a scant few seconds before, and leaned toward him so that her chest, now covered only by the magical leopard-print bra, grazed the top of his head. "Turn to me," she said, again.

"I ... I ... I don't know if I should," he said, quietly, as he turned his head in the other direction. "This is inappropriate," were the words he said, although his mind wanted to say, "oh yeah!!"

"*Não se preocupe.* Don't worry," she purred. He could hear the sound of her pants' zipper being undone, and the sound of fabric against her legs as she stepped out of her shoes and slid her pants down to the floor. From the corner of his eye, he could see them fly onto the chair, in a heap, along with the blouse. "The front door is locked. The Portuguese girl is home. And, you said, you have no appointments." She ran her hand up and down his back. "I trust you. Now you trust me. *Eu não vou contar a ninguém*," she whispered, "that means I won't tell anyone."

She paused, and then added, softly, "besides, you told the Portuguese girl that you were alone for a reason, no?"

He did not realize that she picked up on that comment.

"But," he said after another extended pause, "this is unethical. I can't." He paused again. "Even if I wanted to, I can't." She ran her hand across his body, from the back to his chest, and quickly thrust it downward so that it landed in his lap. Feeling the apparent bulge in his pants, she laughed.

"I think you can. And, Eric," she added, seductively, "I think you want to. *Eu acho que você quer.*"

He slowly turned to her, with her hand still resting atop his bulging crotch. To his left stood Bianca Rodrigues, the beautiful widow Rodrigues, wearing only a sexy, leopard-print bra and the tiniest of pink thongs. She leaned into him, pressing her breasts against his face while she slowly undid the bra hooks. Letting the straps fall down her shoulders, she drew back, slipped off the bra, and asked, "should I do that again?"

Eric gulped. His mind raced. He was her attorney. Of course he wanted her to do it again. But it was improper. Under any reading of the damned ethics rules, he knew it was improper.

He could not enter into any relationship with her, even once. Plus, he remembered, he thought that she killed her husband. What would she do to him if he did engage in some form of relations with her, and then, afterward, did something to upset her? Then she would certainly tell everyone.

His delay worked to his detriment. His logical and ethical detriment, that is. As he was working the different parameters in his mind, she pushed his chair back and gently sat down into his lap. Her thong-clad rear rested atop his now fully-strained pants, her bare breasts resting against his heaving chest as she began to slowly kiss his neck and side of his face. Both of them felt his cock stiffen even more, to the point where he could no longer even bear to have her sitting on top of him in this position. "Please get off," he whispered, "please."

She pulled her lips away from his cheek and looked at him. "If you insist," she answered, struggling to stand as her breasts smacked against his face. "Was I hurting you?" she asked, as she caressed his crotch. "*Eu posso ajudar com isso.* I can help with that." In what seemed like one fluid motion, she undid his belt, unsnapped his pants, and began to slide his zipper downward.

Eric wanted to protest, but he could not. "No … no," he began to say, but then changed to "how?"

She laughed. "You will see," she whispered, as he heard and felt the zipper being pulled to its lowest point and her hand pulling the top sides of his pants apart. He felt the warmth of her hand inside his boxer shorts, as she gently touched the stiff rod, for which she knew that she was fully responsible.

"*Alguém me quer* - Someone wants me," she whispered, almost as if simply talking to herself. "*Posso beijá-lo?* Can I kiss it?" she asked, as she slowly ran her hands up and down the shaft.

Eric wanted to say no, but again, he could not find the strength to deny her. He could not find the strength to deny his pleasure. He felt like he was ready to explode at that moment. He was fucked, one way or the other.

"Yes, please," he answered, as she eagerly placed her warm lips around him. He placed his hands on the back of her head, pulling slightly on her ponytail, as her head moved up and down. He sat in his chair, receiving this special favor from the widow Rodrigues, all the while completely aroused but nervous with the knowledge that he had, potentially, completely compromised his future as an attorney. He opened his eyes and looked downward. He could see the top of her head, and behind it her perfectly-formed ass, clad only in a strip of pink fabric, as she knelt before him. He reached down with his right hand and slid it down the small of her back, grabbing that ass as tightly as he could. For the moment, at least, she was worth it.

CHAPTER XIV

After his tryst with Bianca Rodrigues, Eric was unable to concentrate on his work for the rest of the day. He called Fatima and told her to stay home and, without any matters that needed immediate attention, decided to spend the next couple of hours playing on Facebook and scouring the internet for articles on baseball. He also ran a google search on the name "Joao Rodrigues" to see if there were any articles that contained more information on his death and whether or not the police had uncovered any further evidence, but was unable to locate any.

He went down the hall to the office of his friend and former classmate, criminal defense attorney Jonathan Grant, to see if he wanted to go out for lunch. Grant was surprised to see Eric, especially because, to his knowledge, Eric rarely, if ever, left the building for lunch. "This must be some special day," Grant said as he and Eric strolled out onto Broad Street.

"I guess it is," replied Eric, "it's sunny out, it's summer, and, if we are ever going to get out of the office, this is the day to do it, don't you think?" Eric did not tell Grant that he was smiling because, just a few hours earlier, he had received the best oral sex of his life from his exotic client.

Grant looked skyward. "I guess you're right, Eric. I'm glad that I was able to get out with you." The men turned into a restaurant located on Broad Street, a stone's throw from the courthouse, and nodded to the assemblage of judges seated in a booth near the front window.

"Mr. Goldberg," called Judge Harris as the men passed, "I will be seeing you in my courtroom, tomorrow, right?"

Eric stopped and turned to face the Honorable Frank Harris, one of the judges before whom he regularly appeared on divorce matters. He could not remember if he had court tomorrow, and did not recall seeing anything on his calendar when he checked it that morning. "If you say so, Judge, then yes, I will be there. As always, I look forward to it."

"At least try to sound sincere, Eric," said Judge Steven Dash, seated alongside Judge Harris. "It's not like you are coming to see me, which, of course, is always a pleasure." He laughed, and slapped Judge Harris on the back.

"Of course I am sincere, Your Honor. It is always a pleasure to appear before each of you. Let me correct myself, when I appear before any of you," he said, as he opened his arms to show that he meant all of the judges seated at the table. "All of you enjoy your lunches," he said, before turning and walking to the back of the restaurant to sit with Grant.

"Shit," he said to Grant as he sat, "I had no idea that I had court with Harris tomorrow." He checked the calendar on his phone. There was no mention of a court appearance. He texted Fatima and asked about the next day's calendar. Even home sick, she immediately replied that he had been scheduled for a conference with Judge Harris, but that the conference had been put off for a week at the other attorney's request. "Thank God," Eric said, wiping some sweat from his forehead, "I don't feel like preparing for court tomorrow. I don't feel like doing anything today."

"I know that feeling," Grant replied as he ordered a gin and tonic, "but why so happy today, Eric? It's Monday. Usually you're frantic on Mondays."

Eric asked the waiter for a vodka and cranberry juice, and then turned back to Grant. "I can't tell you. Just suffice it to say that it's been a good morning so far."

"Well," replied Grant, "that is nice and cryptic. I did see a very attractive woman walking into your office this morning when I got in." He paused. "Could she have something to do with it being a good morning?"

Eric smiled. "Perhaps," he answered. "Perhaps it could."

Grant, noticing the smile, grimaced. "Look, Eric," he said, "I don't care what you do, especially now that you're divorced, but you need to be careful. Unless the mere sight of that woman is what made you so happy, you really have to stop."

"I got this one, dude," said Eric. "Nothing improper happened. She's just really hot," he explained, even though he was lying, "sometimes just seeing beauty is enough to brighten my day."

"Alright," Grant groaned, "if you say so."

The waiter brought the men their drinks, and each quickly scanned the menu and ordered sandwiches for lunch. As the waiter turned and walked away, Eric turned to Grant. "Can I ask you a question, Jon?"

"Of course," replied Grant, grimacing. "But I hope it does not involve sex with a client."

"Don't be ridiculous," Eric said, again wiping sweat from his forehead with his napkin. "It's not about that. Well, maybe a little bit." Grant's eyebrows lifted as Eric continued. "What if a client comes on to you? I mean really comes on to you, even if nothing happens? What do you do?"

Grant leaned in closely to Eric so that he could whisper his answer. "There are judges in the room, you ass, why would you ask me that question here?" He took a sip of his gin and tonic. "You know the answer. Get the hell out of there. Do you really want to have ethics charges against you for fucking a client? Seriously?"

"What are you talking about?" asked Eric.

"Come on, Eric," replied Grant, struggling to keep his voice low, "what do you think, I am an idiot? I saw the woman. I know you are talking about her. But just looking at her wouldn't make you that happy. Don't … I repeat, don't, fuck your client!"

"I didn't fuck her," Eric whispered. "She gave me head."

"You've got to be shitting me, you ass. Why are you even telling me this?" asked Grant. "Are you doing it to brag that you got some from her, because I can't think of any other reason that you would even mention it?"

"I don't even know, to be honest with you," answered Eric, "I guess that I just wanted to hear that it was alright."

"Well," Grant shot back in between continued sips of his drink, "I'm not going to be the guy to tell you that. You're walking on very thin ice now. All that she has to do is tell someone and you'll be facing an ethics complaint. Not too bright of you, wouldn't you say?"

Eric thought for a second. While Bianca may have been worth getting involved with for a morning escapade, he did not want to face the ramifications. "You're right," he said sheepishly, "I won't do it again. Can we talk about something else now?"

The rest of the meal was spent with discussions about topics like children and sports, but Eric could tell that Grant was continuing to judge him due to his dalliance with Bianca. The two men then walked back to the office building in silence, and before they retreated to their respective offices, Grant admonished Eric one last time about staying away from his clients.

"And if you do decide to do this again," Grant added, "please do not tell me. As an officer of the court, technically I am supposed to report you for such ethical violations. You have put me in a very precarious situation," he said, as Eric looked at the floor in order to avoid eye contact, "and I am going to forget that we had this conversation."

CHAPTER XV

The next morning, Fatima returned to work and brought Eric a cup of coffee, remarking that it would help awaken him as his reddened eyes betrayed yet another sleepless night. He recounted some of the past day's events to her, carefully leaving out the fact that Bianca Rodrigues had visited and, of course, leaving out the details of her visit. He also did not tell her the reasons why he had not slept the night before – that he had alternatively worried about his encounter with Bianca Rodrigues and longed to again hold her in his arms.

"I need to call the Newark police department," Eric called to Fatima. "Do you know anyone there who can give me some information, or should I just waste my time calling the main number?" He typed "Newark NJ police department" into the "google" box and tried to scroll to the proper number to call.

Fatima appeared in his doorway. "Why are you calling the Newark police department?" she asked, and then paused, as a look of recognition came over her face. "You're calling about Bianca Rodrigues, aren't you? What exactly did I miss yesterday?"

Eric squirmed in his chair, as he sipped from his hot coffee and avoided making eye contact with Fatima. "Nothing. You missed nothing. She called me and asked that I call the police to see what was going on. It's the least I can do, wouldn't you say?"

She looked at him skeptically. "You mean to tell me," she replied, "that a woman who may be guilty of killing her husband called you and asked you to call the police to see if they are still investigating her. And you are doing it. Seriously? I can't believe this."

"Yes, seriously," Eric answered, continuing to fabricate his version of the last interaction between he and Bianca. "Listen, I have her retainer monies," he said, lying to Fatima as he had still never received any monies from Bianca, "and clearly there will not be a divorce action, so I might as well make us some money, no?"

"I guess so," Fatima replied, still showing signs of doubt. "Call the main number. I don't have anyone there who can be of any real help."

"Already calling," Eric said, as he punched out the numbers displayed on his computer screen. Reaching an automated system, he punched the number for "general inquiries" and, after a ten-minute wait, was connected to a live person.

"Newark police, can I help you?" asked the female voice on the other end of the phone.

"Yes," Eric replied, "I am calling to see if I can find out the status of an investigation that I think that the police are doing into a car accident."

"Please hold," said the woman, and Eric heard a clicking sound before he could respond.

"I hate calling f'ing Newark," yelled Eric, "why can't anyone there just do something?"

"You know how it is," called Fatima from her desk. "If you don't want to deal with them, then just don't make the call."

"Very funny," Eric said, and was about to yell something to Fatima when he heard a deep voice through the phone receiver.

"Sergeant Barnes, how can I help you?"

"Sergeant Barnes, my name is Eric Goldberg. I am an attorney in Elizabeth, and am calling to find out the status of an investigation."

"Investigation? Do you mean a drug investigation?" asked Sergeant Barnes.

"No," replied Eric, "I am calling about …"

"You're in the wrong department," interrupted Sergeant Barnes. "Please hold, I will transfer you."

"Shit!!" yelled Eric, as he punched the "intercom" button on his phone and slammed the handset into the receiver. He could hear Fatima chuckling at her desk, and stood up to walk out to her desk. As he reached the other side of his desk, he heard yet another voice ask if they could help him.

"Yes, please," answered Eric with exasperation. "You are the third person that I have spoken to. I am trying to find out about an investigation into a car accident."

"Who are you?" demanded the voice on the other end of the line.

"My name is Eric Goldberg," answered Eric, "and I am an attorney in Elizabeth. I am calling on behalf of a client."

"And who is your client?"

"My client's name is Bianca Rodrigues. Her husband died in a car accident last week and I am trying to find out if the police are looking into the accident or not and, if they are, what they have found out so far."

"Goldberg, you say?" asked the woman.

"Yes, Eric Goldberg," answered Eric.

"That's interesting that you are calling, Mr. Goldberg." Said Detective Loretta Jones. "We were going to be calling you shortly."

Eric could feel his chest start to pound harder. "Calling me?" he asked, "why would you be calling me?" he asked, lifting the handset off of the receiver in order to remove the call from the intercom.

"That I can't tell you," said Detective Jones. "All that I can tell you is that it's about something to do with the vehicle." Hearing Eric's breathing grow louder and harder through the phone, she added, "tell you what, I will have them call you today so you don't have to sit and worry about it. I am sure that it is nothing."

"Uh, uh, OK, thank you" stammered Eric, who could feel rivulets of sweat pouring down his forehead as he hung up the phone. He leaned back in his chair, completely panicked about why the police would be reaching out to him. He felt like he was having heart palpitations, and the sweat was now pouring into his eyes. He wiped his forehead with his left sleeve, and closed his eyes in an attempt to calm himself.

"How did it go?" asked Fatima, unaware of the conversation between Eric and the Sergeant. "Did they give you any information?"

Eric composed himself, wiped the remaining sweat from his forehead, and walked out to where Fatima was sitting. "They, um, they didn't give me any information," he said quietly. "They," he paused, "they want to talk to me."

"Oh my God," yelled Fatima, "why would they want to talk to you?"

"She wouldn't tell me," replied Eric, with obvious concern in his voice. "She's going to have the investigating officer call me later today. Until they do, I think I might have a heart attack."

Fatima rose from her desk, and reached out to grab Eric's hand. "Don't worry," she said, "what could they possibly want to talk to you about, other than that you were representing the woman who they think may have killed her husband? They can't do anything to you."

"I hope you're right," said Eric. Now he was really worried about the fact that he had let Bianca Rodrigues seduce him the day before. What he did not know, at that time, was the reason why the police really wanted to speak with him.

Later that day, Fatima was surprised to see the office door open and two men, dressed in sport shirts and khakis, enter the office. Both of the men wore leather holders which dangled from their belts, and badges were pinned to each of the holders. "Afternoon, ma'am," said one of the men, "My name is Detective Bill Madison, and this is my partner, Detective John Bailey. We are here to see Mr. Goldberg. Is he in?"

Fatima rose from her desk and approached the officers. "Yes Detective, he is," she replied. "May I tell him where you are from and what this is about?"

This time Detective Bailey spoke. "Of course you can. We are from the Newark police department and we are here to ask him a few questions about Joao Rodrigues. He actually called in earlier today, so he should be expecting us," he said, as his eyes darted around the office.

"I think he was expecting a phone call," she answered, "so I assume he will be surprised that you are actually here." She walked toward Eric's office. "Just a second, please. I will see if he is available."

She walked into Eric's office and closed the door behind her. He was sitting, with his back to her, typing furiously on his computer. "I heard them," he said before she could announce the Detectives' presence. He turned to face her. "Do me a favor. Tell them that I am in the middle of something and that I will be out in a couple of minutes."

Fatima nodded, opened the office door, and walked back out to the detectives, both of whom were still standing next to her desk. "He is finishing something up, Detectives, and will be out in a couple of minutes. Please sit," she said, motioning to the chairs near the front door. "Can I get you some coffee?"

Bailey nodded slightly opened his mouth as if to say "yes," but quickly changed his answer to "no" when he saw the disapproving glance that he received from his partner. "No, ma'am," said Detective Madison, "we would rather just sit down with Mr. Goldberg, do what we need to do, and be on our way."

"Thank you. We do appreciate the offer, though," added Detective Bailey," clearly disturbed by his partner's lack of social graces.

The two men sat down, and continued to sit in silence for the next couple of minutes until Eric emerged from his office. Extending his right hand to Detective Bailey, Eric said, "welcome, Detectives. Please come in so that we can discuss whatever it is you need to ask me." He turned to Detective Madison and shook his hand vigorously. "And let me thank you for coming today," he added, "I did get quite a surprise when I called the precinct today and heard that you wanted to speak with me."

Detective Madison looked over at Fatima, seated at her desk to his left, and motioned to Eric's office. "It would be better if we talked in there, sir. May we?"

"Of course," answered Eric, "please do come in." The three men walked into Eric's office, the last, Detective Madison, closing the door behind him.

All three settled into chairs; Eric into his chair and the two detectives into the two seats facing the desk. "You know the reason that we are here, Mr. Goldberg," Detective Madison began, "we are investigating the accident involving Joao Rodrigues. Can we ask you some questions about his wife?"

Eric sat upright in his chair as he addressed the detectives. "Detective," he replied, "I would love to be of assistance in any way that I can, but understand that I am constrained in what we can discuss due to the attorney-client privilege."

"So it is fair to assume that Ms. Rodrigues is your client for something?" asked Detective Madison.

"I really can't say," replied Eric."

"But when you called the office today, you told the person who answered the phone that you were her attorney, didn't you?" asked Detective Bailey, clearly puzzled by his response.

"That's true," Eric said, after thinking about the question for a few seconds. "I am her attorney." He paused, and then continued. "In fact, I do have to tell you that she has retained me to represent her, right? Or otherwise there would be no privilege."

"That's true," answered Detective Bailey.

"You will have to forgive me, then," continued Eric, "we talk so much about the attorney-client privilege that you don't ever want to say anything that could get you in trouble."

"Get you in trouble?" asked Detective Bailey. "That's a strange choice of words, wouldn't you say, counselor? Why would you get in trouble?"

Eric had not realized how bad his declaration sounded until it was repeated by Detective Bailey. He cleared his throat. "You will have to forgive me. It is not often that I speak to Detectives or police in this way, you know, I mean other than when I am bargaining in Municipal Court. So bear with me. What I meant to say is that if we breach the privilege, and say something that was said between us and our clients, then the client can come after us." He pointed to the Law School diploma hanging on the wall. "You can theoretically go home and tell your families about your day, who you spoke with, and so on. We can't. It's one of the reasons that many of us, yours truly included, end up divorced. Lack of communication. Spouses don't understand that we can't talk about things. That's what I was alluding to. I apologize for my lack of proper articulation."

"Well, counselor," replied Detective Bailey, "you are partially right. When we do these investigations, we can't tell anyone what is going on or else we compromise our work. So we are kind of in the same boat."

Detective Madison nodded. "Let's start fresh, then. We established that you represent Bianca Rodrigues. Can we ask what you represent her for?"

"You can ask," Eric replied, "but I can't tell you."

"Can you tell us if she retained you just for the purposes of this investigation, or for something else?" prodded Detective Madison.

"No, I can't, sorry. If I did that then I would be revealing communications between us, which, as we already said, I cannot do."

Detective Madison pulled some papers from a folder that he had been carrying. Handing a stapled group of papers to Eric, he asked, "Mr. Goldberg, do you recognize these papers?"

Eric immediately recognized them. "Yes, detective, I do. This is a retainer agreement between Bianca Rodrigues and me. I think that by reviewing it you can figure out what it was for, and why I was retained."

"Yes, we can," answered Detective Bailey. "So she retained you to represent her for a divorce from her husband only days before her husband ends up dead in a car accident. You don't think that is suspicious?"

"Clearly to you it is," Eric said, "but unless you can find wording in that retainer which talks about how to stage a car accident, I don't know why you are asking me questions. You know that I can't tell you anything about what we may or may not have discussed."

"Let's cut to the chase, sir," barked Detective Madison, who was clearly growing weary of the conversation. "Did she ever tell you that she was going to kill her husband?"

Eric stood from his chair, and walked to the bookcase located to the right of his desk. He pulled a large binder from the second shelf. "Detectives, this is a copy of the New Jersey *Rules of Professional Conduct.* It is here that you find the verbiage about the attorney-client privilege."

"And?" asked Detective Madison, wearily.

"Well, there is an exception to the rule. It states that you can reveal to proper authorities, essentially call the police, if your client threatens to commit bodily harm or worse to someone else and if you believe that they are capable of carrying out such a threat." He paused, and placed the book back onto the shelf. "I am telling you this so that I can then tell you without breaking any attorney-client confidences that no, I never thought that there was any need for me to alert any police or other authorities. You can glean from that statement whatever you want."

Detective Bailey nodded his head slightly. "I will take it to mean that she never told you that she was even thinking of killing or injuring her husband," he said, "is that a fair statement?"

Eric looked at Detective Bailey. "Detective, I can't tell you any more than I already have," he said, as he also nodded his head slightly.

A slight smile creased Detective Bailey's face. His partner, however, was much less pleased with Eric's roundabout responses. "Mr. Goldberg," Detective Madison said, "I get the whole privilege thing. But let me tell you something else. That is not the only reason that we are here. We found a couple of things in the back of the vehicle that may cause you some concern."

"Oh?" asked Eric, nervously. "Please tell me what you are talking about."

"Well," Detective Madison explained, "we found a burned umbrella in the back hatch of the vehicle. Some of the fabric somehow did not burn, and there were letters on it, as if someone had scrawled their name on it in silver highlighter. Just like the one sitting here in this pencil cup on your desk. There were only a few letters, and we could not make out what the entire word was supposed to be, but then, after we discovered the retainer agreement, we were pretty sure that it was your umbrella."

"That's easy to explain," Eric offered up immediately so as not to arouse any further suspicion. "The first night that she came to see me, it was raining outside and she did not have an umbrella, so I gave her mine to use when walking back to her car. I guess that it is true, detective, that no good deed goes unpunished. The fact that I lent her an umbrella should not be a cause célèbre for the Newark police department."

"Normally it would not be," answered Detective Madison, "but there is more. Tucked inside the folds of the umbrella were scissors. You know, scissors that could be used to cut lines in the car, if you catch my drift." He looked at Eric for signs of concern, but could not detect any. "The scissors were completely burned so we could not get prints off of them, we think, but, since they were inside of what you have now admitted was your umbrella, …"

"Detective, please." Eric cut him off. "If you are insinuating that I was somehow part of a scheme to kill Joao Rodrigues, then that is a completely different line of inquiry." He glanced down at his pencil cup. The scissors that had been in the cup were gone. He had not even noticed previously. "Is it possible that she took them?" he wondered to himself. "And I will not answer any more questions," he continued, "without seeking legal counsel of my own. Not that I have anything to hide, mind you, but I don't like the implication. It is one thing to come here and ask me about someone else. It is quite another to begin accusing me."

He stood, and extended his right hand to Detective Bailey. The two detectives also stood. Detective Bailey shook Eric's hand and thanked him for his time. Detective Madison also shook Eric's hand, and advised him that they would be in contact if anything else were to develop. Eric thanked the men for their courtesies, and walked them to the office door. They thanked Fatima on their way out of the office, Detective Bailey again thanking her for the offer of coffee, and left the office. Eric closed the door behind them, leaned against the door, and breathed a heavy sigh.

"Should I even ask what happened in there?" asked Fatima as Eric regained his breath.

"No, not really," answered Eric. In his mind, the less she knew the better. "They were asking me about Bianca and the accident. That's all."

"You seem a little bent out of shape, though," said Fatima, "are you sure that they didn't ask about anything else?"

Eric started to walk back into his office. "There is nothing for you to be concerned with. Hopefully that will be the last of our discussions with the police." He sat down in his chair, looked to the Rodrigues file sitting on the left of his desk, and silently cursed the day that Bianca Rodrigues first walked into his office, the day that she first walked into his life. He reached for the phone to call her and ask her if she knew anything about the Detectives' visit to him, but there was no answer. He was afraid of leaving a message, not knowing if messages or texts would be checked by the police, and hoped that she would see the "missed call" and call him back.

No such return call was received that day, even though Eric kept checking the phone late into the night before finally falling asleep.

CHAPTER XVI

"A lawyer may reveal [confidential] information to the extent the lawyer reasonably believes necessary ... to establish a claim or defense on behalf of the lawyer in a controversy between the lawyer and client, or to establish a defense to a criminal charge, civil claim or disciplinary complaint against the lawyer based upon the conduct in which the client was involved."

- New Jersey Rules of Professional Conduct Paragraph 1.6(d)(2)

Eric spent the next morning in court, appearing before Judge Harris on a case management conference. He ended up sitting in the courthouse hallway with his adversary and their respective clients for two hours, making no progress on settling the clients' differences and finally being released at 11:00, with the admonition that they were to continue negotiating and inform the court by the next week as to any progress.

As he walked from the courthouse to his office, he felt his jacket pocket buzzing, indicating that he had received a text message. Taking his phone from his pocket, he saw that the text was from Fatima – "Get back here as soon as possible. Detectives back again looking for you."

"Shit," Eric muttered to himself as he began to enter his office building. "What the fuck could they possibly want from me now?" Steeling himself as he rode the elevator to his floor, he strode confidently into his office, where Detectives Bailey and Madison were waiting for him. "Detectives," he said as he entered the room and extended his hand to theirs, "I hope that you were not waiting for me very long."

"Not at all," replied Detective Bailey. "We were hoping to be able to speak with you again this morning, if that is OK."

"For you, of course," Eric said. "Let me just go to the men's room and wash my hands first, if you don't mind." He held his hands outward. "I was in court for the past couple of hours, and, to be honest, I hate touching things that many people have already touched so I like to wash my hands once I get back to the office." He looked at Fatima. "Right, Fatima?"

Fatima nodded in accordance as Eric left the office and went to the men's room to wash his hands and to further compose himself. He feared that they had spoken to Bianca and that she had told them of their activities the prior day. He was further concerned that he had not received a call back from Bianca, even though he had tried to call her the previous afternoon. He wet his face with water, dried his hands and face, and checked himself in the mirror. He did not want to appear afraid, even if his insides were churning with trepidation about why the detectives had returned to his office.

Returning to his office, he invited the detectives to join him and each took the same seats as the previous day. The men engaged in small talk, Eric explaining how frustrating his morning in court had been and the two officers empathizing with tales of their own frustrations while on the job. After about five minutes of such chatting, Eric asked, "tell me, detectives, what brings you back here today?"

"Well, Mr. Goldberg," Detective Bailey said, "I know that we were just here yesterday and you told us what you could based on the privilege, but we received an e-mail early this morning that we need to discuss with you."

"An e-mail," Eric asked, puzzled, "what type of e-mail?"

"Believe it or not, an e-mail from Bianca Rodrigues," answered Detective Bailey. "Here's a copy of the e-mail for you to read. As you can see, it makes some fairly strong allegations against you."

"Against me?" Eric asked as he reached for the paper being held by Detective Bailey. "How can there be allegations against me?"

"Read it and then we can discuss," replied Detective Bailey, handing the sheet to Eric.

Eric began to read the e-mail, which was sent to the Newark Police Department:

Dear Sir:

My name is Bianca Rodrigues, and I am the wife of Joao Rodrigues who, as you know, died in a car accident last week. Your office has been asking me questions and treating me like a criminal, and I am being treat unfairly and do not want it to continue.

My children have already lost their father. They cannot lose their mother. I cannot go to jail for something I did not do. I cannot leave my children without any parents.

It is true that me and my husband were not happy, and that I had seen an attorney about getting a divorce. Why would I see an attorney about a divorce if I was going to kill my husband? Wouldn't it be easier to kill him if everyone thought we were happy and then nobody would think I did it? Plus, would I leave my children without a father?

I cannot risk going to jail, so I have taken my children and gone home to Brasil. That way I know we will be together.

I do not know who killed my husband, but believe that it did not happen by accident. There were many people who my husband screwed over in business, and any of these people may be properly checked out. Also, one person who may have done it was my attorney, Eric Goldberg. He told me that my husband was worth more dead than alive when I told him about Joao's life insurance policies, and he also had sex with me even though he knew that I was in bad emotions. He took advantage of me, and it is possible that he killed Joao so that he could share the insurance money. You should talk to Mr. Goldberg about where he was that day.

I hope that you are able to find the person who killed my husband, and will be checking the internet to see when there is an article about your success.

Thank you.

Bianca Rodrigues

Eric's eyes widened as he read the e-mail, especially when he reached the penultimate paragraph. "Certainly you can't believe this," he said to the detectives as he finished and placed the sheet of paper down on the desk in front of him.

"Well, Mr. Goldberg," replied Detective Bailey, "you know that we have to follow up on anything."

"I understand," said Eric, "but certainly you can't believe any of this. The only part that is true is that we made a joke about the life insurance. I do that all of the time, as does every other married person who has life insurance." His voice began to rise. "Quite frankly, if that is enough to accuse someone of murder, then you'd better lock up half the population, if not more." He paused. "And I apologize for getting mad, but this is ridiculous, as I am sure that you can see."

"You admit making the joke?" asked Detective Madison. "Are you then saying that the rest is false, and that you did not have sex with her?"

Eric laughed. "Are you for real, officer? You're asking if I had sex with a client whom I had just met?" His laughter stopped. "Only a fool would risk his license like that."

"You say that," replied Detective Madison, "but I am sure that it goes on all the time."

"Really, you mean like cops do on traffic stops before they let pretty women go?" asked Eric, in a sarcastic tone.

The veins in Detective Madison's neck and forehead began to protrude as his blood pressure grew noticeably higher. "How dare you," he barked, "how dare you ask me that question, and in that tone. Who the fuck do you think you are? We can run your ass down to the station right now if we want to. You should show some respect, if you want to stay out of the holding pen."

Detective Bailey interrupted. "Calm down, Bill," he said quietly. "Let's not let things get out of control here." He turned to Eric. "Mr. Goldberg, I am sure that you understand the sensitive nature of what we are doing here. And no, between you and me I do not believe that a woman who has just fled the country and sent us a note through e-mail is telling the truth. But we have to follow all leads."

Eric calmed himself before replying. "I understand that you guys have to do your jobs, but when you come in here making crazy accusations against me based on the say-so of a woman who, up until yesterday you thought killed her husband, well, think about how you would react."

"I get it," said Detective Bailey, holding his hand in the air so that his partner would know not to interfere. And it looks like you are ready to forget about the attorney-client privilege, which I believe you can do now."

"Actually, that is true," said Eric. He stood and pulled the same book from the shelves that he had previously shown the detectives. He thumbed through the pages, stopping in the middle of the ABA Ethics rules. "Allow me to read the part to you, so that you know that I am still following the rules: '*[i]f a lawyer is accused by his client, he is not precluded from disclosing the truth in respect to the accusation.*' That, detectives, is from the American Bar Association's Canons of Professional Ethics, at Paragraph 37."

"So we are clear, let's break down the e-mail bit by bit, if that is OK with you," said Detective Bailey.

"Let's," said Eric, as he again picked up the piece of paper and began to recite its contents aloud. "The first few paragraphs deal with her and treatment by the police, which clearly I know nothing about." He continued to scan downward. "The only part that deals with me is the last paragraph. She talks about his business associates, none of whom I knew. Then she talks about me. I have already told you about the life insurance joke. Again, it was a joke. You've probably each used it in the past, right?"

Both men nodded. "And you've already denied the sex part, right?" asked Detective Bailey.

"That's right," Eric said, even though technically it was a partial lie. "And I certainly did not take advantage of her in any way." That part was true. If anything, she had seduced him. "And,

I certainly did not kill him to share in any insurance money. Again, I just met her. What kind of crazy scheme would that have been?" That part was also true.

"And lastly, detectives, I was out with friends at a sports bar the night that the accident happened. I found out about it from the newspaper the next day. I can provide you with names if you need them. But rest assured, I was nowhere near Mr. Rodrigues' car. I don't even know what type of car it was."

The two detectives looked at each other and nodded. "Thanks for your time, Mr. Goldberg," said Detective Bailey. "Hopefully this really will be the last time that we have to bother you."

"Yes," said Detective Madison, "but I warn you, if we can get prints off of those scissors, we may be back to get some sample prints from you. Police protocol, you know."

"Absolutely," Eric replied, as he rose and the men shook hands for what he hoped would be the last time before the two detectives repeated their exit from the previous day. He worried, however, that he would be seeing the two men again, and he did not look forward to that day.

CHAPTER XVII

"If a lawyer is accused by his client, he is not precluded from disclosing the truth in respect to the accusation."

- American Bar Association Canons
of Professional Ethics Paragraph 37

After the two detectives left his office, Eric told Fatima that he was going to stop in to talk to Jon Grant for a minute or two. He strode rapidly down the hall, into the office, past Jon's secretary, and plopped down into the chair next to Jon's desk. Grant was on the phone and waved for Eric to wait a minute; Eric beckoned him to end the call immediately, mouthing that he had to talk now.

Jon complied, telling his client that he would call him back later that afternoon. He looked at Eric, and asked, "what's the urgency, pal?"

"No time to joke, Jon," Eric replied. He stood, glanced out the door at Jon's secretary, and closed the door so that he and Jon would have privacy. "Real problems, man, I have real problems."

"Please tell me that it doesn't have anything to do with that blowjob woman from yesterday," said Jon. "Please."

"Wish I could," said Eric, "but I can't." He buried his head in his hands. "The Newark police came to talk to me twice in the last two days. It seems that she has fled to Brazil and is trying to frame me for killing her husband."

"Brazil, huh," Jon said, and then stopped, mouth agape. "Wait a minute," he cried, "did you say that she is trying to frame you for killing her husband? What the fuck is going on with you?"

"Let me start from the beginning," Eric said as his eyes moistened. He told Jon about Bianca Rodrigues, about the car accident that claimed her husband's life, and about how the police found his umbrella and scissors in the car. He told Jon about how Bianca had seduced him and then written a letter to the police detailing not only how they had sex, but also that she believes that Eric had killed her husband. "She said in the letter that she was going back to Brazil so that she would not be prosecuted unfairly," Eric wept, "and I think that this one stick-up-his-ass cop actually believes her." He again buried his head in his hands. "What the fuck am I going to do?"

"Well," Jon replied, "I think you need to figure out a way to clear your name. If you think she did it, then you need to get her to admit it."

Eric raised his head and wiped the tears off of his face. "Sure, but that is easier said than done. How do I get her to confess to someone who matters? How do I even find her? Brazil is a giant fucking country, you know."

"Think for a second. Where is she from? Did she live in one of the cities, or did she come from the country? You can narrow it down. If you were somewhere else and fled to the United

States, everyone would start looking for you in the New York area, right?"

"She said she was Brazilian. I never asked her from where," Eric said, despondently.

"Didn't she come to see you for a divorce? Didn't you ask her the usual questions for the Litigant Sheet? Like place of birth?"

"Shit, that's right," Eric said, bolting upright in his seat. He thought for a second, and a look of recognition crossed his face. "She was born in the city," he cried. "Not Rio, the other one."

"São Paulo?"

"Bingo!" shouted Eric, smiling. "She's from São Paulo!" His smile lessened. "What are there, a hundred million people in that city? How could I find her there?"

"Maybe if you knew someone down there, it would give an outsider like you an advantage," Jon said, smirking.

Eric stared at Jon. "Sure, if I only knew somebody. But who on earth do I know in São Paulo?" He paused. "Oh, that's right. I know nobody in São Paulo. I'm fucked." He leaned back, and buried his face in his hands.

"Not yet, you're not," said Jon. "You may not know anyone in São Paulo, but you did not ask me if I know anyone down there."

Eric stood and placed his hands on Jon's desk, leaning forward to get closer to his friend. "Don't shit me. This is starting to sound like a movie cliché. Do you know anyone down there?"

"Remember my sister Rachel? Her son graduated from Penn State a couple of years ago and moved down to São Paulo. He is living with a Brazilian woman and loving it. His name is Steven. Steven Cooper. I could get his number for you."

"You're serious, right?" Eric pleaded.

Jon nodded his head. "How on earth could I possibly make that up?"

"Then I am going to Brazil." Eric said. "You want to come down with me? At least you could have some fun while I am playing dime-store detective and tracking her down."

Jon clicked on his computer and scrolled down his address list until he reached "Cooper." "Go back to your office," he told Eric, "prepare your office for the fact that you will be gone for a few days, but don't tell Fatima if you know what's good for you. I will call Rachel and get Steve's number. Once you book a flight, we will let him know so he can get you at the airport."

Eric looked at Jon, his eyes again misting. "Thanks so much, man," he said, grabbing Jon in a tight embrace. "I owe you one. Hopefully I make it back here to repay you."

"You'll be fine," Jon assured Eric as the men continued to hug. "And you will buy me lunch when you're back and regale me with tales of the Brazilian women."

Eric loosened his grip on Jon, stepped back, and again wiped his eyes. As he opened the door to Jon's office, he looked back at his friend. "Thanks, man," he said softly, "you really are the best."

"For you, anything," replied Jon, as he watched Eric turn and walk slowly out of his office. He immediately reached for the phone and called his sister so that he could get Steve's contact information in Brazil.

Eric returned to his office, and informed Fatima that he would be going out of town for a couple of days. Rebuffing her attempts at getting information from him, he said simply that he was leaving town for a couple of days and that she shouldn't pry any further. If anything important came up, she should go next door and ask Jon Grant to deal with it. He also told her to make sure not to mention anything to her husband, or anyone else, about his trip.

"This is about the Rodrigues woman, isn't it?" Fatima asked.

"I can't tell you where I am going, or why I am going," responded Eric. "I don't want you to have to tell anyone anything if someone should come here asking questions. This way you can say, with a clear conscience, that you do not know where I am, with whom I am staying, or when I will be back."

The tears welling in her eyes betrayed Fatima's fear and concern over Eric's intended travels. "Promise me that you will be careful, though. Promise me."

"Of course I will be careful," he responded, hugging Fatima as she rested her head against his chest and shoulder. "Don't worry about me, I will be back in a few days and it will be like I never left."

"If you say so," she said, drying the tears from her eyes and cheeks. "I am really worried about you."

"I know, and I appreciate it," he replied, turning to walk into his office. He finished up a couple of things that were lingering on his desk, and then left the office at 3:30, heading home to pack for his trip to Brazil. "I love you," he said to Fatima as he walked out of the office.

"Love you, too," she called as he closed the doors. Tears again welled up in her eyes, and she sat down at her desk, sobbing, praying that he would return safely.

Eric arrived home to an empty apartment, and was able to throw a week's worth of clothes and necessary items into a suitcase and carry-on bag in the span of a half an hour. At 5:30,

Jason strolled in and noticed the bags sitting in the hallway. "What's up dad?" he called out, "going somewhere?"

"Yes," Eric answered, walking out from the kitchen. "I have to go away for a few days."

"Seems awfully cryptic, dad," Jason said, "do you think you could tell me where you are going and, more importantly, why you are going somewhere on such short notice?"

"Wish that I could, son," Eric said, placing his hand on Jason's shoulder. "Just trust me. I need to take care of something and won't be back for a few days. I don't want to worry you with any details."

A look of concern came over Jason's face. "But dad," he protested, "now I am concerned. Are you in some kind of trouble? What am I going to say to mom when she finds out that you went away and didn't even tell me where you were going?"

Eric again tried to reassure his son. "Don't be concerned. I am not in any trouble. I am just trying to take care of a situation before it becomes a possible problem. And don't worry about your mother. I will deal with her when I return." He paused. "I think I should be back in about four days, but it might be a little longer. If it will be longer, I will be in touch."

"Will I be able to reach you? If I need anything, I mean."

"I will have my cell phone with me," Eric explained, "but I don't know if I will have service or not where I am going. Try me if you want; if I have service, I will answer. If not, then I will reach out to you once I do have service."

"Alright, dad, I trust you. Don't screw anything up." Jason looked into the kitchen where his father was standing when he arrived home. "Is there dinner for us?"

"No," Eric answered, "I had bought some stuff for you for the next few days and wanted to make sure it was all put away. I figured we would run out and get a quick bite to eat before I left."

Jason nodded his approval, and the two men walked to Eric's car. They drove to a sushi restaurant and ate dinner, with no further conversation being had about Eric's trip or the reason for the trip. When they returned home afterward, however, Jason went into his room and emerged several minutes later. "Dad," he said, "I know that we have not spoken all that much since the divorce, and I know that my anger and need to work things out is responsible for a lot of our problems." A tear formed in his eye. "But Dad, I am really worried about where you are going. Are you not telling me where because you're mad at me?"

"No, son, not at all," Eric responded, taken aback by his son's concern and display of emotion. "This has nothing to do with anything that has gone on between us. It's just something that you can't know. Fatima doesn't know either."

"Really?" Jason asked, "I mean, because I would hate to think that something happened to you and we were never able to, you know, make up and be cool with each other again." He began to cry. "I need you, dad."

"And I need you, Jason," Eric said, tears of his own forming in his eyes. "Don't worry, I will be home soon and then we can hang out all you want. Come July, when you have no classes, I will take some more time off and we will do some stuff, OK?"

"Sure," Jason said, drying his eyes. "Please promise me you'll be careful."

"You sound just like Fatima, you know that?" Eric replied. "Don't worry, I will be safe. You're not getting rid of me that easily."

"Good," Jason said. "And by the way, you should be glad that Fatima cares about you so much. We're all you've got, you know." He paused. "But let me tell you something. You having me and Fatima is more than most other people have. Don't forget it."

Eric looked at his son and smiled before sweeping him up in a bear hug. He thought about what Jason had said, and began to realize that maybe things were not so bad after all. "Look what I can learn from my son," he said, "maybe I have raised you pretty well."

"Maybe you have," Jason said as he turned and walked toward his room, "but you're not done yet, so you have to come home." He walked into his room and closed the door. Eric, allowing his son's parting words to reverberate through his mind, sat down on his bed and cried.

CHAPTER XVIII

Before Jason had arrived home, Eric had managed to book a flight leaving for São Paulo the next morning. It was an expensive ticket, and he had to fly out of JFK airport in New York City rather than his preferred Newark Airport, but Eric needed to get there as soon as possible. He immediately telephoned Jon Grant, who promised that his nephew would be at Guarulhos Governor Andre Franco Montoro Intl. Airport in São Paulo to meet him.

The next morning, he took a taxi to JFK, and waited in the terminal for two hours, nervously drinking two cups of coffee, before boarding the plane for the almost 4,800 mile flight to São Paulo. He spent the first three hours of the flight studying the sights and landmarks of his destination city, trying to figure out every possible place where he could locate Bianca Rodrigues. Exhausted by his efforts, he fell asleep somewhere over the Atlantic Ocean, awakening as the plane began its final descent into the airport.

Hearing the flight attendant giving instructions in both English and Portuguese, the trip, and its purpose, suddenly became real to Eric. "What am I doing?" he asked himself, "I must be out of my mind." Twenty minutes later, the plane touched down, and taxied closer to the terminal. The passengers, including Eric, stepped off of the plane and all walked, en masse, to the baggage claim where Eric expected to see Steve Cooper waiting for him.

As he approached the baggage claim area, however, the person holding a sign bearing the name "Eric Goldberg" most certainly was not Steve Cooper. Rather, the person holding the sign and waiting for Eric was an almost six-foot vision of exotic loveliness, a leggy, obviously native Brazilian wearing a short, white skirt and a navy Penn State T-shirt. The shirt was gathered at the side and its knot secured atop her left hip by what appeared to be a large rubber band. The bottom hem of the shirt rested millimeters above the top of her skirt, allowing Eric to catch a glimpse of her perfectly-toned and tanned stomach as she stood, waiting. Approaching the woman carefully, Eric cleared his throat before announcing his presence. "Excuse me, but I am Eric Goldberg."

The woman smiled and leaned in to hug Eric. He was somewhat taken aback by her forward move, but figured that if we was going to have to hug someone, it may as well be his new Amazonian friend. "So pleased to meet you," the woman said, "my name is Leticia Alves. I am Steve's girlfriend. He was stuck at work today so I have the privilege of picking you up and bringing you home." She kissed him on both cheeks before releasing him from her grip.

"Sounds great," said Eric. "It's really so nice of you to come out here to get me."

"It's nothing, really," said Leticia in an almost lyrical tone of voice. "It's only about 20 miles to home, which should take us about two hours."

"Really," Eric asked, "two hours?"

Leticia laughed. "Well, maybe not. Let's say about an hour and forty-five minutes, maybe more depending on traffic."

Now it was Eric's turn to laugh. "Here I thought I was leaving the Jersey traffic behind. Where do we go to get my bag?"

"To the left," Leticia said, as she turned and started walking toward the baggage carousel. Eric followed closely behind, but not too closely so that he could best enjoy the sight of Leticia Alves walking in her short skirt.

The two retrieved Eric's bags, and walked to Leticia's car, Eric rolling his large suitcase behind him and Leticia carrying his smaller bag. The temperature in São Paulo was slightly cooler than he had left behind in Elizabeth, as Brazil was entering its winter season. The sun shone brightly as they walked, however, providing Eric with a feeling that his efforts at finding Bianca Rodrigues would prove fruitful.

Turning to Leticia as they walked, he apologized for taking up her time. "I hope that you didn't have to take off from work to pick me up, Leticia."

"No, I didn't," Leticia answered. "I just graduated from college last year and am working on my masters for teaching. I have been working as a substitute teacher at the local school while I finish getting the degree. School's out now, so I am home anyway."

"You're a substitute teacher?" Eric said, "my schools sure didn't have substitute teachers as attractive as you when I was a kid."

"Well," Leticia answered as her cheeks turned a brighter shade of pink, "maybe that's because you grew up in the United States and not here in Brazil."

"That can't be it," he replied, "because if all teachers looked like you, nobody would learn anything. Especially, I would say, if you were teaching high school. There is no way any of those boys would be concentrating if you were standing in front of the class."

Now Leticia's face was bright red, both from the sun and Eric's comments. "Luckily, then," she said, "I teach young kids. They're in first and second grade. They are not as distracted by me."

"Maybe so, but wait until you become a real teacher and not just a substitute. Then you will see how many of the fathers want to come in for the parent-teacher conferences. We had a teacher like that when my son was in school, Ms. Stevens. She was about your age, I guess, about 24…"

"I am 22, thank you very much," Leticia shot back.

"I must be over-guessing because you seem so mature," Eric said, drawing laughter from Leticia. "Anyway, all of us dads went to conferences that year. Some of the guys had never even been in the school before. And Ms. Stevens, well, she played it up well. She would wear skirts only a little longer than the one you have on now, and sit with her legs slightly open to give the guys a show. The women didn't like it much, however, and for the next couple of years the women would not let their husbands go the conferences. I don't know what she wore for the class during the day, but for conferences she was, as they say, dressed to kill."

"A skirt a little longer than mine," said Leticia, "that doesn't seem so bad."

"Maybe not here, but up there it was a minor scandal."

They reached the car. Leticia pushed a button on the remote and the trunk flew open. Eric lifted both bags into the trunk, and the two entered the vehicle, Eric fishing for his wallet so that he could pay the parking fee when they exited the lot. As she sat, Leticia moved her legs slightly apart, so that the white of her underwear was visible between her legs. "Is this what that Ms. Stevens used to do in class?" she asked.

"What?" Eric replied in response to Leticia's inquiry, too busy fumbling for his wallet to see her pose.

"I said," Leticia repeated as she spread her legs wider, "is this what that Ms. Stevens used to do in class?"

Eric took some money in one hand and placed the wallet back into his pocket with the other. He looked over at Leticia, and for the first time noticed that her legs were spread at a 45 degree angle, providing him with a clear shot of her lace-covered crotch. "Some … something like that," he stuttered, shocked by the display being put on by the woman he had met only minutes before.

"Well," she answered, "then maybe I should try this in class. Maybe it would get me more work."

"Maybe she would get more work?" Eric thought to himself, thinking that with looks like that, she could be teacher of the year in some people's eyes. "You never know," he said, "anything is possible." He handed her the money, insisting that he pay for the parking, as she brought her legs to a more normal position and drove the vehicle out of the lot and onto the highway that would take them home.

Almost immediately after leaving the airport parking lot, however, they encountered heavy traffic on the *Marginal Tiete*. The highway, which offered views of the Tiete River and downtown São Paulo, was, as Leticia explained, the main road from the airport to the city, and was the main road from one side of São Paulo to the other. "How about we listen to some music?" Leticia asked as they slowed. "Open the glove compartment, and take out the CD which has the letters "GG" on it," she instructed.

Eric opened the glove compartment, and shuffled through the stack of CD's until he found the one with the "GG" printed in black marker. "Here you go," he said as he handed the CD to Leticia. She pushed the CD into the vehicle's stereo, and the familiar reggae strains of *"No Woman, No Cry"* filled the car. "Ah, Bob Marley," Eric said, as he leaned back in his seat and closed his eyes.

"Wait a minute," Leticia cautioned. "Don't be too sure. Things aren't always as they seem, Mr. Goldberg. I would think that you, a lawyer, would know that."

Eric was puzzled by her comment, until he realized that it was not Bob Marley's voice singing. "Now I'm confused," he replied.

Leticia laughed. "Don't be confused. All that you need to do sometimes is pay more attention to what you are seeing or hearing, or stop before you say something. This is Gilberto Gil.

He's covered many Marley songs." She paused to let Eric listen to the music a bit longer. "My dad used to listen to him. Enjoy."

As they were talking, Eric again noticed his driver's beauty. Her long, lean legs went upward from the car's pedals and seemed to disappear into the car seat, as her short skirt rode up to the point where it was nearly non-existent. He caught himself staring at her legs, which she had so proudly displayed when they first entered the car, and quickly looked away before his gaze was discovered. Looking out the window, he asked, "so tell me about this road? Someone told me that it often rains in Brazil. Does the roadway flood?"

"All the time," Leticia answered, "the river rises when it rains too much and covers the highway. I don't know why they don't do anything to stop it, but I guess that is part of its charm."

"Where are the soccer stadiums?" Eric asked, "I would have thought that we would have passed one by now."

"Soccer?" Leticia asked in a demeaning tone. "What is this soccer?" She looked at Eric and shook her head slowly. "You are in Brazil, sir, and the word is '*futebol*'."

Eric looked at her sheepishly. "I'm so sorry, Ms. Alves," he said quietly. "Might I ask when we might see a *futebol* stadium?"

"I'm so glad you asked, even though your accident is terrible" she replied, smiling, a broad smile that could light up not only a room, but an entire football stadium, thought Eric. "We will see one soon. There are a few major football teams here in São Paulo. You may have heard of them – São Paulo FC, Corinthians, Palmeiras."

"I have heard of the first two. Didn't Pele play for São Paulo?"

"No," she said with a disappointed tone, "he played for Santos, also based out of São Paulo. But he was a little before my time, you know."

Now it was Eric's turn to take a sarcastic tone. "He was before my time also, you know. I'm not that old."

Leticia laughed again. "I did not say that you were, although you are clearly older than the 24 that you guessed for me before. I would guess that you are in your mid-40's, right? So that would make you old enough to be my father or my husband, depending on which part of the world you are raised."

"Guilty as charged," said Eric, "but we are getting off-topic. Stop flirting with me and tell me about a football stadium," he added, using the American pronunciation of the word "*futebol*" to avoid further heckling.

"Flirting?" asked Leticia, "now it is me who is guilty as charged." She looked at Eric and winked. "You know how Brazilian girls are, right? Certainly you have heard stories."

Eric looked at Leticia with uncertainty for a moment, until she burst out in laughter. "Funny," he said, blushing, "can we please go back to what we were talking about?"

"Of course we can," she said, gently rubbing his leg with her right hand, "the biggest stadium is Morumbi Stadium. That's where the São Paulo team plays. It seats about 68,000 people or so, but once, I am told, there were about twice as many people crammed in there for a game."

"Normally I would want to see a game while I was here," Eric lamented, "but I can't even think about it. I need to stay focused." He stared pensively into the distance, watching the São Paulo skyline unfold before him as they drove.

Leticia glanced over at Eric, and debated whether or not to interrupt his moment of introspection. She saw him draw a deep breath, and decided to ask her guest the reason for his visit, and the reason why he had to, in his words, stay focused. "Eric," she asked, "do you mind if I ask you why you are here in Brazil? Steve didn't tell me anything, just asked me to pick you up at the airport."

Eric sighed deeply. "It's a long story," he answered. "It is a very long story."

"Then this is the perfect time to tell me," said Leticia, chuckling lightly, "look around you. The traffic is terrible. We will be stuck together in the car for at least another hour, and I don't know if I can flirt with you for that long without you telling Steve and getting me in trouble." She again stroked his leg. There was an uneasy silence, which signaled to her that he did not want to discuss business at that moment. She decided to ease his mind. "But seriously, you don't have to tell me if you don't want to."

Eric looked at Leticia, and took her hand in his. "You want the quick version? I messed up. I messed up big." Leticia nodded, as if to prod him to continue. "I am here because I am trying to find a woman. A woman who I think killed her husband. And the reason that I am here is because she is trying to frame me for it, and I need to clear my name because the local police were not going to do anything about it."

Leticia squeezed his hand in a reassuring manner. "Well, we are here to help you. Steve spoke to his Uncle Jon, who said that we should do anything we can to make things easier for you." She paused. "But I am a little confused. How did you mess up? She killed him, right? Why would anyone believe that you did it?"

Eric looked away from Leticia as a tear formed in his right eye. "That's not important right now," he answered, "all that is important is that I find her and get her to confess. I will tell you more later." He wiped the tear from his cheek. "But if I have someone as beautiful as you to help me out, then I am really quite lucky," he said, as the traffic on the *Marginal Tiete* came to a grinding halt.

Leticia's cheeks again turned a bright red, and she took her right hand and swept her hair over her shoulder. "Thank you, Eric," she said, and, keeping her foot firmly on the brake, turned her legs slightly toward Eric, leaned over and kissed him on the cheek. Moving her body back into its proper driving position, she then turned the volume knob to the right, and the sounds of Gilberto Gil's version of Bob Marley's *"Three Little Birds"* wafted through the car. "And we are here for you. Just like the song says, don't worry about a thing. Every little thing," she paused, "is gonna be alright."

"I sure hope so," Eric said, quietly, "I sure hope so."

CHAPTER XIX

The phone was ringing as Steve Cooper put the key into the front door of his apartment. Rushing through the doorway, he reached for the phone and clicked "on" just before the fourth ring. "Hello," he said, breathlessly, "hello?"

"Steve, my boy," answered the voice on the other end of the phone, "how is my favorite Brazilian nephew?"

"Funny, Uncle Jon. Things here are fine." He walked over to the door, removed his keys from the lock, and threw them into a small bowl located on a table next to the door. "Are you checking to see if your friend got here?"

"Yeah, I wanted to see how his flight was. I didn't want to call him since I assume he is all wound up, so I figured I would try you."

"Leticia went to the airport to get him," Steve answered. "They aren't home yet; the traffic from the airport must be insane at this time of day. I assume they will be here any minute."

"Do me a favor, OK, just call me when he gets there." Jon said. "Don't tell him that you are calling me. I am just a little worried about him."

"That's what you said yesterday when you told me he was coming down," Steve answered, "but you did not tell me why he was coming down. Can you give me a little information so we can be of help to him?"

"I assume he will tell you the whole story tonight," Jon replied, "but here is a brief overview." He proceeded to tell Steve what Eric had told him about Bianca Rodrigues, from their first meeting up through the letter that she sent to the Newark Police Department.

"So let me get this straight," Steve said, recounting what he had just heard. "This woman comes into his office to retain him for a divorce. Her husband ends up dead a couple of days later. She comes back to his office afterward, blows him, and then sends a letter to the cops blaming him for setting up the accident that killed her husband. Does that sum it up well?"

"Sadly, yes," Jon replied, "and now he is coming to you so that he can find her and clear his name. I just want you to make sure that you are all safe. And call me when he gets there, don't forget."

"You got it, Uncle Jon. I will call you in a little while."

"Thanks, kiddo. I knew I could count on you. Treat him as if it were me. He and I go a long way back, about 20-some odd years, since law school. Talk to you later."

Steve thumbed through the mail that he had carried up from the downstairs mailbox, and changed from his work clothes to a more casual t-shirt and jeans. He was scanning the contents of the refrigerator looking for something that they could make for dinner when he heard Leticia and their guest in the outer hallway.

"*Estamos em casa, meu amor*," Leticia called out as she opened the front door. Turning to Eric, she apologized for speaking in Portuguese and quietly repeated herself in English. "We are home, my love."

"I heard you in the hallway," Steve called from the kitchen. "I will be right there."

"Let's just put your bags here for now, Eric," Leticia said, we can put them into the extra room later. "He's in the kitchen. Hopefully he has opened a bottle of wine for us to drink." She started to walk to the right. "Come with me," she said, taking his hand.

Steve appeared in the archway which separated the front of the apartment from the kitchen. He walked to Eric and extended his hand. "Mr. Goldstein, welcome to Brazil. My uncle speaks very highly of you,"

Eric let go of Leticia's hand and took Steve's hand in his, and as the men shook hands he replied, "and you as well. I can't tell you how much this means to me that you are taking me in. Hopefully I will not be here for too long and won't get in your way. And please, call me Eric."

"You're not a bother at all," Leticia said as she leaned in to Steve and kissed him. "Now you two chat while I get cleaned up." She turned to walk to the bedroom. "No offense, Eric, but I always feel dirty when I go the airport and take that long drive back. I will be back in a minute. You can feel free to clean up also, if you want, the bathroom is right over there," she said, turning and pointing to the right. She walked slowly to her room, the two men watching her hips swivel as she tugged at the rubber band on the side of her shirt to undo its knot.

Eric turned to Steve. "I will wash up in a bit. Thanks again for having me here. I don't know what Jon told you, but I will fill you in soon." He paused and looked around the apartment. "Nice place you have here," he added, "and you are really lucky to have a girlfriend like Leticia. She's a lovely girl. And she's funny, too. You don't usually find that combination, so hang onto her."

"Like she said, no problem with you staying here," Steve answered. "My uncle told me a little about why you are here, and we are going to help you as much as possible. As for Leticia, yes, she is great," he looked to the bedroom door to make sure that she was not coming back into the room, "but … how can I explain this?" He paused. "You know how we have the perception in the U.S. about Brazilian girls and their wildness?"

"Yes," Eric replied, "why?"

"Well," Steve continued, "you will see when you are here that most aren't like that. My girlfriend, however, seems to be. She is very flirtatious and, sometimes," he looked skyward, as if searching for the proper word, "a bit of an exhibitionist. And some men probably like that. They like to show off their girlfriends or wives. I am not. It's taking some getting used to."

"I understand what you are saying," Eric whispered, even though he really did not see the problem, "but I am thinking that you are exaggerating a little. Maybe it is just a cultural difference, and you are down here, don't forget. You know what they say, 'When in Rome,...'"

"I know," said Steve, "but it still bothers me. Not enough to break up with her, but I am hoping that she calms down a little as we go forward." He gazed at a picture of the two of them. "But I shouldn't bother you with my problems, right? You are here for a reason, which is, based on what little I know, far worse than a girlfriend who likes to hug other men. So for me, I will stop complaining because other than that, to be honest, things are perfect."

"Steve, *meu amor*, don't give Eric any problems," Leticia called from behind the bedroom door. "Pour us some wine so we can sit and chat before dinner."

"*Claro, meu amor* (of course, my love)," Steve called back. "*Não se preocupe com isso*." He whispered to Eric, "I am telling her not to worry about it, and now I will ask her if she wants red or white wine." Raising his voice again, he called to Leticia, "*vinho tinto ou branco?*"

"*Tinto*, of course," Leticia answered, as she emerged from the bedroom. Barefoot and clad only in her Penn State t-shirt, which now hung mid-way down her thighs, she walked over to where the men were standing. "Now I feel much better," she said, hugging Steve as Steve looked over at Eric as if to say that her manner of dress proved his point. "See how clean I am," she added, as she squeezed Steve so tightly that he lost his balance and they tumbled to the floor.

"Let me help you guys up," Eric laughed as he leaned over and extended his hand to assist the fallen pair. As he leaned, he noticed that Leticia had fallen on top of Eric. Her t-shirt had been pulled up during the fall, and her thong-clad, perfectly-formed rear was staring him in the face.

"Take my hand," Leticia said as she rolled off of Steve, her thong-covered crotch now in full view. "Leave him on the floor," she added, making no attempt to lower her shirt until Eric helped her to a standing position. "Pardon my, how would you say, appearance," she whispered to Eric as she ran her hands down her shirt, "I certainly did not expect to fall like that."

"It's OK," Eric whispered back in an attempt to diffuse any embarrassment that she may have been feeling, even though he did not detect any, "now you can walk around the apartment in your underwear as much as you want because I have already seen it."

She chuckled lightly. "I will think about it," she replied, in a more normal voice, and walked into the kitchen. "Stay tuned," she added.

Now Eric extended his hand to Steve and helped him up off of the floor. "You have to excuse my girlfriend, Eric," Steve said, "she tends to be a little over-affectionate at times."

"You are a lucky man," Eric replied, looking at Leticia as she bent over to look into the lower cabinet for a bottle of red wine, her shirt again riding up her back to expose the bottom of her thong. "Take it from one who has been divorced and has not been able to find the perfect one," he added, "if you find her, hang on to her."

"I know," said Steve, who was looking in the other direction so he was unaware of the fact that Eric was admiring Leticia's backside, "but I just don't know if she is the one. For the reason I told you about before. I guess that time will tell."

"Steve," Leticia called, "where is the corkscrew?"

"I left it on the counter in there," he replied. "Don't you see it?" He turned to Eric and whispered, "plus, she's not always the brightest bulb."

"If that's her biggest problem, my friend," whispered Eric, "then you are doing just fine."

"Found it!" she called, "go sit down on the couch, boys, *vou levar o vinho.*"

"She just said that she would bring us the wine," Steve clarified for Eric. "She likes to teach me Portuguese whenever possible. It's actually easier to learn when you do phrases instead of just learning words, so I have picked up a lot since we have been together."

"That's great," Eric replied as the men sat, Eric on the couch and Steve on a chair to the right of the couch. "I have been listening to Portuguese in my office for years, but am unable to speak more than a couple of words. It is a very difficult language to learn." He paused as Leticia's beauty again filled the room, this time carrying two glasses of red wine, and then added, "then again, maybe I am just too old."

"Too old for what?" asked Leticia as she handed the glasses to the men.

"To learn the language," Eric responded. "As you get older, it gets harder and harder. I think that I am past the point where I can even absorb the words."

"Don't be silly," Leticia said as she turned to the kitchen and went to retrieve a glass of wine for herself. "You will see. Stay here with us for a few days and you will be amazed at what you can learn. *Não e certo, meu amor?*"

"Of course you are right," Steve called to Leticia as she poured herself a glass of wine. "Aren't you always?"

"Claro", she replied as she walked back into the room and sat on the couch alongside Eric. "Of course I am."

"I just realized, I have to make a phone call," Steve said. He had forgotten to call his uncle when Eric arrived and wanted to make sure that he called before he started to worry. "Please excuse me for a minute." He walked into the bedroom, closed the door, and told his uncle that Eric had arrived and that everything was fine.

Leticia crossed her legs so that her left was over her right, and her left foot moved slowly up and down in a rhythmic motion as it faced Eric. The two sat, sipping their wine in silence, until Leticia spoke.

"Are you going to tell me why you are here?" she asked, "you know that we can't help you without knowing what we are supposed to be doing."

Her straight-forward manner caught Eric by surprise, although he was starting to get an idea of what Steve had been talking about earlier. "I will," he said, "in a little while. Can we just sit and enjoy the drink first? It will calm me down so that I can tell you everything properly."

She nodded her approval, and sat back, her foot brushing against Eric's leg as she reclined further. Steve re-appeared in the room. "Call is done. No more work for today, guys." He looked into the kitchen. "Let's finish this drink and go out for dinner."

"I don't want to be a bother," Eric protested. "There is no need to go out. If we do, though, I insist on paying. Surely they will take my dollars, right?"

"Don't be so sure," Steve replied. "The strength of the dollar, as you know, is not what it used to be."

"Don't get in the way, *meu amor*, of course we can go out if he is paying." She placed her glass on the table in front of the couch and reached over to hug Eric. "If our *Americano* wants to take us out, who are we to argue?" She wrapped her arms tightly around Eric, draping her left leg over his.

"Come on, Leticia," Steve cried, "leave the man alone." He looked at Eric. "We already planned to take you out, somewhere where you will hopefully feel comfortable. And I will be paying. You can get tomorrow night, if you want."

Leticia jumped up from the couch, the back of her shirt flying skyward and providing Eric with another quick view of her thong-clad rear end. "I will go get dressed," she declared, "and listen to Steve, we are paying."

"If you insist," Eric replied. "I really don't want to be a bother, though."

"Not a bother at all," said Steve, "it is our pleasure. Finish your wine and," he started to raise his voice so that it could be heard in the next room, "we will go once *Princesa* Leticia is ready."

"I heard that," she called from the next room. "Don't you want me to look *bela* for our dinner in *Bixiga*?"

The two men looked at each other, each understanding the word "*bela*". "But you already look beautiful," they said in unison, as Leticia made her entrance back into the room, wearing a dress which, by what Eric considered to be her standards, was actually quite conservative, a floor-length blue dress accented with a large white belt. Her hair was swept up into a ponytail, with a large blue circle of fabric keeping it in place.

"How about now, boys, am I *bela* now?" she asked, posing with her right hand to her outwardly-extended hip.

"*Naturalmente*," replied Steve, as he walked over to kiss her.

"I would agree," said Eric, as he finished his glass of wine. "By the way," he asked, "what is *Bixiga*?"

Steve turned back to him. "Oh, that is our 'Little Italy' section," he replied. "We thought that the trip would be easier for you if you had some American Italian comfort food on your first night." He lowered his voice to a whisper. "Plus, to be honest with you, I love it and she doesn't let me go there that much so it is a treat for me."

"*Não é verdade,*" she argued. "That's not true." She looked at Eric. "Well, the first part is. The second isn't." She walked toward Eric and again took his hand in hers. "Let's go, Eric, we can leave this *idiota* here." Now she looked back at Steve. "*Tchau, ex-namorado,*" she said, as she locked her right elbow with Eric's left and strode toward the door.

"You just said 'goodbye, ex-boyfriend' to me," Steve replied, "That's kind of cold, even for you, don't you think?"

By now Leticia was laughing uncontrollably, and had to lean into Eric to avoid falling down as her body convulsed. "*Talvez* (maybe), so let's go. I've had enough of talking. I am getting hungry." She stroked Eric's arm with her free left hand. "Aren't you, *o meu novo amor*?"

"*Meu amor* was my love, right?" Eric asked. Leticia nodded. "And *novo* must mean new. I'm your new love?" He looked at Steve and shook his head slowly. "Sorry, buddy. You know how it goes."

"Will the two of you please shut up?" Steve pleaded. "One glass of wine and I am surrounded by idiots. Can we please just go to the car and get to the restaurant? Now I am hungry. There is a big plate of pasta calling my name."

As the three walked down the hallway of the apartment building and descended the two flights to the parking lot, Eric's arm still entwined with Leticia's, he felt at ease. More at ease than he had felt in some time. If Steve and Leticia were trying to make him feel welcomed in Brazil, they were certainly succeeding.

The drive to *Bixiga* took less time than Eric had expected, especially after what seemed like an interminable ride home from the airport. Because it was still early by local standards, the three were seated immediately upon their arrival at the restaurant. They all perused the menus, which were in Portuguese with English subtitles. Each placed their order with the waitress, Eric mispronouncing the Portuguese phrase for chicken parmesan – *frango parmegiana*. Each agreed to split a bottle of wine, although Eric suspected that it would simply be the first of several.

When the waitress walked back to the kitchen to place their order, Eric asked the others if he could explain the reasons for his intrusion into their lives. They both agreed, and Eric told the story. He talked about Bianca Rodrigues, about how she had come to see him for representation, about how he had given her an umbrella due to the rain the evening of their first meeting, and about how she had taken his scissors without his knowledge. He told them about the car accident, and how Bianca had sent a letter to the police blaming him and how she had fled to Brazil, supposedly to protect her children. He did not mention their sexual encounter, for fear of having them, especially Leticia, think any less of him.

"Wow," Steve said when he was finished, which coincided with the three finishing their first bottle of wine. "That is some story. How do you know that she is here in São Paulo?"

"To tell you the truth," he answered, "I don't. I only know that she is from here, and logic dictates that she will come back here." He paused, and looked around to make sure that nobody else was listening. "I don't think that she will go to her family, though, that is too easy. That is why it won't be easy to find her. Any assistance will prove invaluable."

Leticia motioned to the waitress to bring another bottle of wine. "Don't worry, Eric," she said, "we will help you."

"This is where Leticia will come in very handy, much more than I would," added Steve. "I would suspect that a woman in her thirties, as you described, who just got rid of her older and controlling husband, would be like the proverbial Catholic School girl when she leaves home for the first time…"

"*Desculpa-me*," Leticia interrupted. "Excuse me, but I went to a Catholic School when I was living in Miami. What exactly do you mean by that?"

"What he means," Eric said in order to help Steve, "is that she will want to live the wild life that she has been missing for so long, like how people who go to strict schools, like Catholic Schools, will sometimes get in trouble when their restraints are taken off." He looked to Steve, who nodded in agreement."

"Oh," she answered, "I understand. But let me tell you, I never lived as strictly as that."

"Why do I believe that?" replied Steve. "I can't even imagine you at such a school." He placed his hand on her leg, "although I can picture you in a catholic schoolgirl outfit. That would be very nice."

"Keep dreaming," she said. "The way you are going, you are looking at sleeping on the couch tonight." She poured everyone a fresh glass of wine from the new bottle and turned to Eric. "I can be of help. I know the clubs here. I know where the young people like to go. If you guys are right, then she is going to try to act like she is younger." She smiled. "Like me."

The waitress returned with their food. Three steaming hot plates of classic Italian food sat on the table, and the three started to eat, all of their minds whirring with how they would try to locate Bianca Rodrigues.

Three meals, two bottles of wine, and three cappuccinos later, they again got into Steve's car and drove back to the apartment. Once inside, Leticia pulled fresh towels from the closet, handed them to Eric, and pointed him to the room where he would be sleeping. She also pointed to a bathroom down the hall which would be his alone to use. The room's freshly-made bed beckoned to Eric, and he told them that he had to get some sleep, as he was exhausted from traveling, and thanked them again for their hospitality.

"Our pleasure," a tipsy Leticia replied, kissing him on both cheeks. "Now get some sleep. We have a busy day of planning tomorrow."

"She's a woman on a mission now, Eric," added Steve. "Get ready, because there will be no rest tomorrow."

"Thanks again, guys," Eric replied. "I will sleep better knowing that I have your help." He walked into his bedroom. "Good night, see you in the morning."

Steve and Leticia walked into their bedroom as Eric closed the door to his room. He took off his shirt and pants, putting on a pair of shorts to sleep and pulling his toiletry bag from his suitcase. He also hung some shirts on hangers he found in the closet so that they would not be overly wrinkled. He opened the door and went to the bathroom to brush his teeth and wash his face, pausing to look in the mirror while asking what he had done to get himself into this predicament.

Walking back to his room, he encountered Leticia in the hallway. She had changed her clothes, and was now wearing a faded Yankees' t-shirt which had the sleeves cut off and which only reached down to her navel. He could see from the open sides of the shirt that she had removed her bra, and there was at least a two-to-three-inch gap between the bottom of her shirt and her thong underwear. He stopped, surprised, when he saw her.

"I'm sorry," she said, "I surprised you?"

"Yes," he replied, "I thought you had gone to bed."

"I will, in a moment. I just wanted to say one more thing to you. Actually, I wanted to say two more things."

"Sure," he said, "I am all ears."

"First," she said, her words still slurring, "I want you to know that we will find this woman for you. Don't worry about it. We will find her and make sure that everything is cleared up."

"Thank you," he replied, "that is comforting to me. And what is the second thing?"

"Isn't it *óbvio*?" she said, placing her hands on her hips and leaning to Eric so that their faces were now a scant few inches apart. "I thought about it."

"About it … about what?" he stammered in confusion.

"Don't you remember? You said that I could walk around in my underwear if I wanted." She moved her hands down and snapped the sides of her thong. "I decided that I would do it." Now she took her hands and grabbed Eric's arms, pulling him closer as she again kissed him on both cheeks. "Just something for you to think about," she whispered. She let go of his arms and turned to walk away. "*boa noite*, Eric. "*Doces sonhos.* That means sweet dreams."

"Uh, you too," he said, as he watched Leticia walk toward her bedroom, her body shimmering in the moonlight that sneaked in through the apartment's windows.

As he placed his head on his pillow, Eric thought not of Bianca Rodrigues and his quest to find her. For the first time in a week, he was not thinking of her. Tonight, he went to sleep thinking of Leticia Alves, thinking about her laugh, her smile, and, of course, her perfect body.

As he drifted off to sleep, Bianca Rodrigues laid her head on a pillow only two miles away. "*Eu te disse, meu amor,*" she whispered to the man lying next to her. "I told you we would get away with it, my love. Once we sell the house and also have the insurance money, we will be set for life." She laughed lightly to herself, confident in her belief that she would not be implicated in her husband's death and unaware of the fact that Eric Goldberg, and the potential spoiling of her plan, was so close to her.

CHAPTER XX

The next morning, Jose Neto awoke to the sound of his girlfriend's slow, rhythmic breathing. She had just come to stay with him a couple of days ago, and they easily picked up where they had left off when she had returned to the United States after her last visit, almost four months ago. Back then, he was carrying on an affair with an older, married woman. The circumstances this time were completely different. This time, there was no husband for her to go home to. Also, last time it was just the two of them. Now, his girlfriend's two daughters slept in the next room, completely unaware of the circumstances under which they found themselves back in São Paulo.

Jose quietly slipped out of bed, pulled on some shorts, and walked out into the hallway. Tiptoeing into the adjoining room, he shook his head when he saw the laptop computer and clothes that littered its floor, all of which bore testament to the fact that children were now living with him in his apartment. He normally lived alone in his two-bedroom home, an apartment with a small kitchen and only one bathroom. For a single man, the apartment was a palace. With four of them there, however, space was rapidly becoming increasingly scarce. He knew that his girlfriend and her girls could not live with him for long, but her promise that she would share her newfound wealth with him, the monies that would be coming from the insurance companies, would enable them to purchase a larger home together.

He wondered if he was ready for an instant family, or if he was capable of acting as a surrogate father for the two girls, whose father had recently died in an accident. The older girl was ten. He was only 22, certainly not old enough to properly parent children; his older girlfriend had recently turned 31, so she was about his age when her daughter was first born. He had met her two years ago when she was visiting São Paulo, a week when she left her husband and children behind in the United States and tried to recapture her youth in her native country. He, at the tender age of 20, was captivated by her beauty and the ability to learn from her sexual experiences and aggressiveness; she leapt at the chance to be the dominant half of a relationship, she explained, her will having been broken time and again by her domineering husband.

They had several more trysts over the next two years, the last two of which contained discussions of her leaving her husband so that they could be together. When it became apparent that money would be tough to come by and that she was facing the loss of her children to her publically well-known and well-respected husband, the two of them hatched a plan to erase him from the picture. A few days ago, his girlfriend had carried out the plan that she and Jose, a mechanic by trade, had crafted. He knew that she had no problem committing adultery, but he was surprised, and perhaps a little scared, that she could so easily participate in someone's murder.

As he looked around, worried about how his future could be with such a woman but at the same time smiling as he envisioned a larger living space, he heard her voice call to him from the hallway. "Jose," Bianca Rodrigues called in a sleepy voice, "*volta para a cama. Esta cedo, eu quero dormir mais um pouco* (come back to bed. It's early, and I want to sleep some more.)"

"*No, meu amor, é 8:00,*" he called back to her, quietly, in order to not awaken the children. "I'm not coming back to bed. It is not early. Usually I am up earlier than this for work." He had been studying and practicing his English in anticipation of moving to the United States once his girlfriend was free to marry him and allow him to emigrate legally. He did not know, however, if this chance would ever come based on comments that she had made upon returning to his apartment those scant few days earlier.

These were the points where they differed greatly. She relished the thought of going back to Brazil and speaking only Portuguese, having grown tired of a bi-lingual lifestyle, but Jose wanted to use his English as often as possible. She wanted to forget that she had kids and live like she was his age, unencumbered by responsibility, and he wanted to mature and act more like an adult. He did not know, however, if an instant family was the proper way for him to mature. It was something that he clearly had not thought about thoroughly during her last visit.

He heard her soft footsteps approaching and then felt her naked breasts pressed against his body, as her arms ran up and down his equally bare chest. "Bianca, the girls may wake up," he said, as he looked back over his shoulder, "don't you think you should put some clothes on?"

She took his right hand and ran it up and down her rear end, so that he could feel the fabric of her bikini underwear. "I'm not totally *nua*," she answered, "*Estou usando a roupa de baixo*. (I am wearing underwear.)" She released his hand and turned, then taking his hand again and covering her breasts with their intertwined arms. "Besides, now my chest is covered too. And the girls are used to seeing my body, so there is nothing to worry about."

He pulled his arm away and stepped back. Bianca placed her arms in front of her chest in mock embarrassment as he shook his head. "But they have not seen your body, or so much of it, *comigo* (with me) or *com outro homem* (with another man). Their father has been dead for a week. How do you think they would react to this?"

She paused, but he did not wait for an answer.

"I don't want to find out," he added, in a stern voice, "*por favor va colocar uma roupa*. Please put on some clothes."

Bianca flashed back to one of her last fights with her dead husband, when he called her a *prostituta* and made a similar demand for her to put clothes on. There, he did not want the neighbors to see her body clad only in underwear, as opposed to Jose's fear of the children walking in on them. Whereas she raged at Joao Rodrigues, a man who she despised, for making such a comment, however, with Jose Neto, her lover, her reaction was markedly different. She looked at him sheepishly, uncrossed her arms and stood there. "I am going to start to think that you are growing tired of my old body already."

"That's not it," he responded, "your body is fantastic. You look like a teenager. But with the girls here, we should be more careful."

She smiled, raised her arms, and reached out to hug him again. "*Para você, querido*. For you dear, I will put some clothes on." She walked back into the bedroom to get dressed, while an exasperated yet visibly aroused Jose again wondered if he had stepped into a dangerous situation.

At the same time that Bianca Rodrigues was getting dressed in order to ease her boyfriend's concerns about others seeing her without proper clothing, Leticia Alves awoke with a slight pounding in the front of her head, no doubt the lingering effects of the previous night's wine consumption. She stumbled out of bed, heard water running in the bathroom, and assumed that Steve had already showered and was shaving in preparation for going to work. Slowly walking to the kitchen, she fumbled through the cabinets for the coffee maker. Filling it with water and coffee grounds, she stood, leaning against the countertop, holding her head in one hand as she waited, eagerly, for the coffee to brew so that she could try to squelch her headache.

Steve emerged from the bedroom, dressed for work in his suit and tie, and saw Leticia standing in the kitchen dressed only in her belly t-shirt and thong. He gasped audibly, causing her to look in his direction. "Leticia, seriously," he said, "we have a guest. Don't you think that you should put some clothes on?"

Leticia looked down at her bare stomach and thong-clad crotch, and shrugged her shoulders. "*Sinto muito, meu amor*," she croaked. "I'm sorry." She walked toward him. "I forgot," she added, lying, and also not telling him that Eric had seen her dressed, or undressed, depending on one's perspective, in these very clothes the night before. She had told Steve that she was going to make sure that the front door to the apartment was locked when she left the room last night, and never mentioned that she and Eric had spoken, much less that she had made sure that Eric would see her dressed in such a provocative manner. "I will go put something on. You stand here and pour the coffee when it is ready."

Steve poured two cups of coffee, adding milk to each and two teaspoons of sugar for Leticia's, as she returned to the kitchen.

She was now wearing one of those microscopic whisps of clothing that the youth of today calls shorts in addition to her t-shirt. "Is this acceptable?" she asked, as she reached for her coffee mug.

Steve looked at her and sighed. "I guess so," he said sadly, "but I would have preferred something a little longer. I don't like when you wear those shorts. The bottom part of your ass sticks out." She started to respond, but he cut her off. "I know, I know. This is how everyone wears them. But it doesn't mean that I have to like it."

With her first sips of coffee coursing through her veins, Leticia felt infinitely more coherent than she had a scant few minutes ago. "*você ama esses shorts curtos, admita*" she replied. "You love these shorts. Admit it."

"No, I don't," he replied, "*ama-o*. I love you, but I don't love the shorts."

"But you love me. That's the important part," she said, sweeping him up in a hug. "You're going to work now?"

"Yes, I have to. I have a meeting this morning but should be able to come home a little after *meio-dia*. If you two leave the house this morning," he cautioned her, "please be careful. We can do real searching after I get home." He quickly gulped down his coffee, kissed her goodbye, and left the apartment. Leticia took the rest of her coffee and walked into the living room, sat on the couch, and waited for Eric to awaken so that she could start the search for Bianca Rodrigues.

Eric emerged from his room approximately five minutes later. He had been awakened by the muffled sounds of Steve and Leticia talking, but had stayed in bed in a futile attempt to get some additional sleep. He also was suffering from a hangover, and prayed that the smell of coffee that he detected was real and not a figment of his imagination. Putting on a t-shirt, he walked into the living room and said to Leticia, *"boa manha."*

"A good morning to you, Eric," she replied, "you're so cute, trying Portuguese." She stood and approached him, placing her arms around him and kissing him on his cheeks. "We will work on your pronunciation later," she added, laughing. "Would you like some coffee?"

"Naturalmente," he replied, using one of the words that he had picked up from listening to Leticia the previous evening. "But what do you mean we will work on my pronunciation? I thought I said it pretty well."

"I didn't say it was bad," she said as she poured his coffee. "I just said we should work on it … to make it *perfeito*, or, as you would say, perfect. Now stop complaining. Do you take *leite e açucar* in your coffee?"

"Yes, please. I will take both milk and sugar. I like it when the Portuguese words sound just like Spanish." He looked around the apartment. "Where's Steve?"

"He had to go to work this morning, but will be back here a little after noon. He told me that we should be careful without him this morning, but I assume that you are as anxious to start looking for her as I am so we can do whatever we want."

The fervor with which she wanted to begin searching for Bianca both pleased and scared him. Of course he wanted to find her as soon as possible, but he also knew that they had to be careful so that they were not discovered. If Bianca knew that he was looking for her, then she could really disappear. And then his best chance at clearing his name would be gone as well. But it would be wrong to squelch Leticia's enthusiasm. "You bet. Let me just drink some coffee first to get rid of this hangover."

"You too?" she asked, "my head was pounding. Here," she said, placing her arm around his waist, "come and sit with me in the living room." They both walked into the next room, sat on the couch, drinking their coffee as the warmth of both the coffee and the sunlight streaming in through the windows above the couch enveloped them.

"One thing to remember, though," he said as they sat, "I can't let her see me before I see her. If that happens, she's gone. So we have to be very careful."

"*Naturalmente,*" she replied. "But here's a problem. I assume you don't have a picture of her. How will I know when I see her? Can you describe her?"

Eric chuckled at the irony of her last question. He had envisioned Bianca Rodrigues in his dreams for the past week. He could recall every inch of her body, from the hair that he noticed at their first meeting to the beautiful sight of her thong-covered rear end as she pleasured him at their last meeting. Literally, he could visualize her from top to bottom. Describing her, however, in recognizable terms to Leticia? He did not know how he could do that. "I want to say that I can," he said, slowly, "but for some reason I am having trouble." He paused. "I could say that she looks Brazilian, but that's not going to do much good here, will it?"

"No," Leticia said, laughing. "Let's try it this way. I look Brazilian to you, right?" she asked. He nodded. "Then let's compare her to me, so I at least have an idea of what she looks like. You said she was in her mid-thirties, right? So that would make her what, about ten years older than me."

Eric thought for a second. "She's thirty-one," he recalled. "So yes, she is a little less than ten years older than you."

"It's a start. How about her hair? Is it like mine?" She put her coffee mug on the table and put both of her hands on the back of her neck, under her hair, and lifted them quickly so that her hair spilled over her shoulders. Her hair was wavy, but not nearly as curly as Bianca's. It also was not as long, although its color, even the highlights, reminded Eric of Bianca's.

"A little," he replied. "Her hair is curly. Not, what do you call them, ringlets, but curly, certainly more than yours. And it is a little shorter than your hair, but the color is the same. And she is much shorter than you. I think she is about five-foot two or three. What are you, about five-nine?"

"Five-foot ten," she corrected him. "I'm only a little shorter than you. And if I wear my heels when we go to the clubs, then both you and Steve will be shorter than me." She paused. "It bothers him sometimes. I don't know why. But now we are going off-topic. So we know about hair and height. What about her eyes? What color are they?"

Eric was embarrassed to admit that he did not recall her eye color. He struggled to remember what he had written down in his papers. "What are you, a police sketch artist?" he asked, laughing, attempting to buy some time before admitting that he could not place her correct eye color. "I'm trying to remember," he said, "so many people from South America and Latin America have brown eyes," he added, "but for some reason…"

"I don't have brown eyes, or hadn't you noticed?" Leticia interrupted. He looked at her, and gazed into her sparkling hazel eyes. He hadn't even noticed the color before.

"You didn't let me finish my sentence, *meu amor*," he said, sarcastically. "What I was going to say is that Brazil is different. There were so many transplanted Europeans here that many of the people have light eyes, so it is much different from the rest of South America. And by the way," he added, "I did notice your eyes," he was now lying, "and they are a beautiful shade of hazel."

She blushed. "Points for you," she said, "now what about her eye color?"

"Light brown," he suddenly recalled. "They were a very pale brown. Not a typical dark brown color."

"Now we are getting somewhere. Five-foot two or three, hair my color but curlier and shorter, and light brown eyes. How about her body?" Leticia asked, arching her back slightly so that her breasts were more evident. "Describe it to me."

"Seriously?" Eric asked, "I don't know how to … at least not tactfully."

"What do you mean, tactfully?" replied Leticia.

Eric paused before answering. "I … I mean," he stammered, "I don't want to say anything improper or offensive."

"It takes a lot to offend me, Eric," Leticia said, "and, I might add, you've seen most of my body. I have not been embarrassed about that, right?" she pulled at the side of her t-shirt, exposing part of her left breast and the outer edge of its nipple.

"Certainly you can describe someone else's to me in terms that won't, as you said, offend me."

Eric averted his gaze from her exhibitionism. "Let me get this straight," he croaked, "you want me to compare her body to yours? You've got to be kidding."

"Not at all," she said, leaning closer to him. "I know you saw her naked," she whispered in his ear.

"How ... how ... how do you know that?" he asked, shocked.

"Because," she explained, "I know my people, at least some of them. They will do anything to get what they want. And you are a smart guy, yet she got totally inside your head. The only way that she could do that is by letting you have sex with her. Or, more likely, she was the aggressor." She paused. "Am I close?"

"No, not really," he lied in response. "I didn't have sex with her," he added, adhering to the Bill Clinton definition of the term "sex".

She looked at him skeptically. "But you saw her naked, I am certain of that."

Now he was trapped. He had denied it the previous evening, yet somehow Leticia made him want to tell her the truth now, even though it would, in his mind, make him look like a sleazy guy. Yet here she sat, basically exposing herself to him, and he had not taken any action with her, nor did he intend to, so she could not think that he was a complete snake. Plus, if he expected to have her help, he had to be honest with her. If she thought he was lying or hiding something, she would not risk her health to help him. "Sort of," he replied.

She laughed. "Sort of? What kind of answer is that? Either you did or you didn't." She stood. "I need to use the bathroom and will be right back. While I am gone, think about what you meant by that answer." She walked to her bedroom.

Eric was starting to sweat. He did not know if it was from the heat of the sunlight beating down on him, or from the intense interrogation that he was being subjected to by Leticia. Usually he was the interrogator, and he did not enjoy being on the other end of a stream of difficult and prying questions. Regardless of the reason, however, the sweat was no doubt becoming noticeable on his forehead. He would have to tell her the truth when she came back.

She returned two minutes later, minus the shorts that she had put on to please Steve. She stood in front of Eric, put her hands on her hips, and asked, "Eric, as you can now see and hopefully appreciate, I am wearing a t-shirt and underwear. Is this quote, sort of naked, unquote, in your definition?"

Now the sweat was running down his forehead, and he had to wipe some stinging droplets out of his left eye. "Uh, not exactly," he answered.

"Oh, then let's try this," she replied. She lifted the t-shirt over her head, holding it in her left hand, and stood before him, wearing only her thong. "Well, how about now? Is this sort of naked?"

Eric closed his eyes so that he would not stare at Leticia's body. "Yes," he said quietly. "Please put your shirt back on so I can open my eyes."

"OK," she answered. "Give me a second. And I knew it. Don't lie to me again, Eric, or you will be sorry. I don't like being lied to." She paused, and he heard the movement of fabric. "You can open your eyes now," she said, as he felt the movement of her sitting on the couch next to him.

He opened his eyes and looked to his left, intending to apologize to her. The first thing he saw, however, was her naked breasts buoyantly hovering approximately two feet from his eyes. Her shirt lay in a ball on the chair to her left, and her hair had all been brushed back off of her shoulders so that his view of her breasts was completely unencumbered. "I thought you said you were putting your shirt back on," he cried, again closing his eyes. "Now I feel uncomfortable."

"Well," she said, "you lied to me. I lied to you." He could feel her moving closer. "Now describe. I need to know what we are looking for."

Eric was at a loss for words. He could not possibly describe someone else's body, in comparison to Leticia's, without somehow getting himself in trouble. "Like yours," he said, "only about ten years older."

"Not good enough. She's shorter than me, right? Let's talk about the rest. How about her chest? Is it bigger than mine or smaller?"

"I don't know," he replied, eyes still closed.

"Yes you do," she said, "I know you felt hers. Would it help if you felt mine?" Her voice sounded closer, and he could feel her presence directly beside him.

"No and no," he said, turning the other direction.

"I don't believe you. What did I say about lying to me? What did she do, rub up against you with her chest? Like this?" she asked, as she placed her body alongside his, his left shoulder snug between her breasts.

"No," he gulped, "she did not do that."

"Or was it more like this?" she asked, as she maneuvered her body so that she was straddling him, the pores on her breasts stiffening as his breath forced air against them. His lack of response did not go unnoticed. She pushed herself against him, so that her breasts flattened against his face. "Or like this?"

Eric pushed her away, moved to his right so that he could release himself from her grip, and quickly stood. "Yes," he said, "it was like that. But I am not playing this game anymore. Her breasts are bigger than yours. Your stomach is flatter. Your ass is smaller. Are you happy now?" He grabbed his coffee mug from the table and walked into the kitchen, running hot water through the mug to wash out any remaining coffee and leaving the mug in the sink.

Leticia followed him into the kitchen. "Yes, I am. Now I know what we are looking for. Turn around and look at me."

"No," Eric replied.

"Seriously," she demanded, "turn around and look at me." Her voice hardened as she repeated her instruction in Portuguese. "*Olhe papa mim.*"

The last time Eric had heard those words, he had turned to see an almost-naked Bianca Rodrigues standing beside him. Fearful of what he would see this time, he slowly turned and saw Leticia standing before him. Thankfully, she had put her t-shirt back on, and had her arms extended as if looking for a hug. Eric stood at the sink, and did not move forward into her waiting arms. She waved both hands in an inward motion, as if to beckon him into her arms. He still refused to move.

Leticia sighed and moved forward, wrapping her arms around Eric as he stood, stiffly, by the sink. He looked down and could see the small piece of fabric that separated the two halves of her backside, the same view that he had of Bianca Rodrigues only days earlier. The symmetry between the woman who accused him of murder and the woman who was going to save him from that woman was not lost on him. Crazy, these Brazilian women are, he thought.

"I'm sorry if I offended you, Eric," Leticia said. "I don't want you to feel uncomfortable. I just needed for you to give me the information so I could help you, and you weren't going to unless I did something crazy." She let go and took a step back. "Listen," she continued, "I don't want to have an affair with you, so don't take what I do the wrong way. I love Steve. I am not going to do anything to mess that up."

"I am glad to hear that," Eric replied, "apparently I misunderstood a couple of things. I apologize for the confusion but I think you can see where I would take things incorrectly."

"Don't worry about it. I told you before, things aren't always as they seem. Now I am going to take a shower. Leave the mugs in the sink, and I will take care of them later." She walked back to the table, fetched her coffee mug, and placed it into the sink. "You get dressed – shower if you want, and then let's sit down and formulate what we are going to do today."

"Sounds good to me," Eric said with a sigh of relief. "I think I will shower. I will need about 20 minutes to get ready."

"Then you will be waiting for me, of course," Leticia said. I will need a little longer." She turned and started to walk to her bedroom, removing her shirt again as she was halfway down the hallway. Again turning to Eric, her breasts staring at him, she said, "my ass is smaller than hers? Thanks for the compliment." Seeing him now staring at her breasts, the sight that he had so scrupulously avoided before, she added, "welcome to Brazil. This is what we are like."

Eric averted his eyes, and started down the hallway just as Leticia entered her room, beginning to pull her thong off as she closed the door halfway behind her, almost daring Eric to peek inside. He instead quickly turned into his room and sat down on the bed, his growing manhood betraying his efforts at not objectifying Leticia as being sexy. Contrary to what Leticia had just said, Eric started to think, things often were exactly what they appeared to be. Leticia clearly loved life and was, to put it mildly, a "free spirit." He could appreciate that part of her. As for her continued exhibitionism, however, he would have to be very careful so as not to create any problems between he, Leticia, and Steve. That would be extremely bad, especially if word were to reach Jon Grant up in Elizabeth.

CHAPTER XXI

Fatima was seated at her desk when she heard a knock at the door. Before she could answer, the office door opened, and Detective Bailey stepped inside. Fatima looked for Detective Madison to follow, but it became apparent that Detective Bailey was alone when he closed the door behind him. "Detective Bailey, if I recall," Fatima said, "to what do I owe the pleasure of your visit today?"

"I was hoping you could be of some help to me," Detective Bailey responded, "it involves, as you may imagine, your boss."

"If you are here to see him, Detective, I am sorry," Fatima said sweetly, "he is not here today."

"Please," he replied, "call me John. I know that Mr. Goldberg is not here today." He paused and looked over his shoulder, as if he expected someone to walk in behind him. "That's why I am here, to tell you the truth."

"Really?" Fatima queried, her voice decidedly more downcast than before. "How do you know that is not here, John?" It felt strange to Fatima to be calling the Detective by his first name, but at the same time she felt comforted by his presence and the fact that he desired for her to be so informal with him.

"The Police Department was informed that Mr. Goldberg flew to Brazil yesterday, because it appears that his name turned up on a flight roster to São Paulo," he explained. Fatima's gasp signaled to Detective Bailey that she was unaware of Eric's travels. "I assume that he did not tell you where he was going. He is a smart man, and no doubt did not want to get you involved in this."

"What do you mean by 'this'?" Fatima questioned.

The Detective took a deep breath. "The belief in the department is that Bianca Rodrigues and Eric Goldberg plotted the murder of Joao Rodrigues together," he began to explain. "It is further the belief of the department that her letter was an attempt at obscuring the plot between the two, to allow her to establish a position in Brazil where he would later join her. At some point it is expected that all of the life insurance monies that Joao Rodrigues possessed will be transferred to a secret account in Brazil, so that the two of them will not be traced. By trying to frame Mr. Goldberg, the department believes, Ms. Rodrigues was trying to make sure that she received all of the insurance monies, which we believe were fairly substantial."

"John," Fatima pleaded, "certainly you don't believe this. You can't believe that Eric was involved in this." She started to cry. "He's not just my boss, you know," she said, wiping tears from her face. "He's also my family."

"I know," Detective Bailey replied, as he took a tissue from the box on Fatima's desk and handed it to her. "That's why I am here. I don't believe that he was involved. Maybe I am crazy, but I believe what he has told us."

"Thank you," Fatima cried, both for the tissue and his words of confidence about Eric.

"My pleasure," he said. "Now, my belief is that he went to Brazil on some kind of half-cocked vigilante mission. I need for you to contact him and tell him to stop."

"Why?"

"Because the Newark P.D. has been in contact with the Federal Authorities, who are contacting their counterparts in São Paulo seeking their cooperation in apprehending both Bianca Rodrigues and Eric Goldberg. While it is no secret that getting someone extradited from down there is not an easy task, they may be looking for him soon."

Fatima took a deep breath and sighed. "Let's assume they do find him. I assume that he will take the worst of the brunt from the Brazilian police since he is not from there, whereas she is a native and they will make things easier for her."

"Exactly my thoughts," Detective Bailey replied. "I can't say for sure, but if I had to make a bet, that is what I would say will happen." He paused. "But there's more."

"Shit," she said, quickly apologizing for her use of the expletive. "I am so sorry that I used that word, John, it is not ladylike, nor is it professional." Tears again welled up in her eyes. "What more is there?"

"Someone is putting a great deal of pressure on the chief to get those two back from Brazil," he explained. "I don't know who, but I can tell you that there will likely be a press conference over the next couple of days where the chief identifies Ms. Rodrigues and Eric as being involved in a conspiracy to murder her husband. While it will be embarrassing to the police that both of them are in Brazil, perhaps together, at least our department will save face by saying that it has identified suspects. I don't think Eric wants that happening, so if he comes back or at least evidences an intention to come back I think that the chief will change his mind."

Tears were now streaming down Fatima's face. "But John," she cried, "I don't know if I can even reach him. I will try, but I don't know if I will be able to. Can you ask the chief to hold off for a couple of days?"

"Honestly," he said, looking downward, "no. I am not even supposed to be here. That's why I am here without Madison. Nobody can know that I was here. Just try to get hold of him. I can't promise that it will all work out if he comes back, but I know it will be worse if he stays down there. Here's my card. Call me if you need anything."

"OK," she sniffled, "I will try. Will you let me know if anything else does happen?"

"I will try, Fatima," he answered as he walked to the door, "but I can't make any promises. I trust you understand."

"I do," she replied, "and thank you Detective Bailey, I mean John. I really appreciate it."

"Just doing what I think is right. Now you stay safe, OK? You've got a family to worry about," he said, pointing to the picture frame on her desk. He opened the door, stepped into the hallway, and quickly closed it behind him.

Fatima sat at her desk, trying to compose herself, and cursed Eric for putting her in this situation. A ringing phone echoed through the office, but Fatima was in no condition to speak to any clients or adversaries at that moment so the call went unanswered. After several minutes, during which she dried her eyes and assured herself that Detective Bailey was gone from the building, she went down the hall to Jon Grant's office.

Entering the office, Fatima spoke to Jon's secretary, Paula Lopez, and asked to see him. He heard Fatima's voice from inside his office and beckoned to her to come in. Once she entered the doorway, he could see her reddened eyes, feared that something had gone horribly wrong, and motioned for her to close the office door behind her. She obliged, sat down in the chair opposite Jon Grant's desk, took a deep breath, and began to recount what had transpired in her office only minutes earlier.

"So the detective came to you and told you to have Eric come back from Brazil," Jon said, repeating part of what Fatima had told him, "interesting. Do you believe him, or do you think that there is another reason why he came to the office?"

Fatima thought for a second. "I honestly don't know. I mean, he came alone and sounded sincere, but I do not know if we can totally believe him, obviously."

"And you have no idea where he is," Jon stated, looking directly into her eyes, "right, Fatima?"

"That is correct, Jon," Fatima answered, "but I have a sneaky suspicion that you do," she added, a faint smile creasing her lips.

"Think all you want," he replied, "but you thinking it does not make it so. I suppose, however, that there is a way that I could get in touch with him. Can you do one thing for me, though?" She nodded in agreement, and he continued, "if in fact there is going to be a press conference where they announce that Eric was a conspirator, someone will have to get hold of Jason ahead of time and let him know what is going on, at least the most basic part. He can't find out where Eric is through the papers. And I assume you should also tell your husband, so he can do damage control within the family if needed. I wouldn't worry about Eric's ex-wife, though. We don't want to give her any ammunition if the matter is never publicized."

"I can do that, certainly. What else do you need from me?" Fatima asked.

Jon pondered the question for a moment before answering. "I can't think of anything now, thanks. Just try to make sure that whomever you tell, whether Jason, Bruce, whoever, keeps it to themselves. We can't have this information out there. It would ruin Eric, and we can't run that risk."

"You got it," Fatima answered, standing and leaning over the desk to kiss Jon goodbye. "Thank you so much. You've made me feel so much better. These last few days have been killing me."

"He's lucky to have someone like you who cares about him, you know," said Jon. "He talks about you all the time, about how fortunate he is that you married his cousin and work for him. He'll make sure he comes back just to see you, and, of course, Jason. So don't worry. It will work out."

"Do you really think so?" Fatima asked as she opened the office door and stepped into the outer room.

"Of course," Jon answered, although he was beginning to have doubts of his own. When he heard Fatima say goodbye to Paula and close the outside door behind her, he again closed his office door and raced to his desk to call Eric.

CHAPTER XXII

Eric and Leticia were in the car, driving to the *mercado* to pick up some snacks and other food for the apartment to eat while they were plotting their night's activities. Before going to the store, Leticia had taken Eric on a hour-long, mini-tour of the part of the city between Mooca and downtown São Paulo, traveling through the neighborhood where she had grown up. She pointed out her old school, the playground where she spent much of her childhood, and, as they approached downtown, an office building that Steve and his firm were in the process of renovating. Eric engaged Leticia in conversation about all of these sights, but at the same time made sure to keep his eyes out for any glimpse of Bianca Rodrigues. Despite his efforts, however, there was no sign of her.

As they approached the *mercado's* parking lot, Eric was surprised to feel his cell phone buzzing in his pocket. Reaching into the pocket, he pulled out the phone and saw the name "Jon Grant" on the screen. Clicking the phone on, he answered, hurriedly, "Jon, what's wrong? Why are you calling me?"

"Sorry to bother you, Eric. How are things going there so far?"

"Good, thanks. Leticia and I are in the car, going to the market to pick up supplies."

"Leticia? Isn't she a doll?"

Eric looked at her direction and smiled, knowing that she could likely hear Jon's booming voice through the phone. "Yes, she is," he answered, as Leticia began to blush and called out to say hi to her favorite almost-uncle.

"Tell her I said hi back, and that I miss her special hugs." Eric repeated Jon's comment, and then returned to the call. "Listen, Eric," Jon said, "the reason for my call is that Fatima came into the office today. Apparently you had a visit from one of the Newark Detectives today."

"Was it that asshole, Madison?" Eric asked.

"Don't think so," Jon answered. "The way she talked about him, he sounded like the 'good cop' half of a 'good cop-bad cop' duo."

"Then it must have been Bailey," said Eric, "what exactly did he say to her?"

"The quick version is that the cops think you are in Brazil with Bianca Rodrigues," said Jon, loudly enough for Leticia to hear and causing a frown to form on her face. "They think that the two of you planned this out together, that her letter was a smokescreen to let her get away, and that the two of you are somehow planning to collect the insurance money."

"Really? Did he say that he believed it? Shit, does Fatima believe it?"

"No to both, it seems," Jon replied. "Bailey said he came in because he believes you and wanted to help you out, and Fatima definitely does not believe it. She is really worried about you."

"She's great," Eric said, "I really am lucky to have her, just like Jason said before I left, and I have taken her for granted. I feel terribly putting her through this."

"Well, she's being a trouper. So this Detective also told her that they were in contact with the Feds, and that they were allegedly contacting the authorities in São Paulo to arrest both you and Bianca and send you back up here."

"They are talking about extraditing each of us from Brazil?" Eric said, laughing. "They're kidding, right?"

"No, that's what he said," Jon said, sternly, "but I am not as concerned with that as with what the fuck can happen to you if they get you. The pretty Brazilian woman, they're going to be nice to her. The guy from the United States, though, he's gonna get the shit kicked out of him."

"You think so?" Eric asked.

"I know so," Jon replied. "Right, Leticia?" he yelled into the phone.

"You know it, Uncle Jon," Leticia yelled back. "But don't worry, because we are taking good care of him. And from what he says, I am prettier than this Bianca woman so the police will be nice to him as long as he is with me."

"Eric," Jon said in a quieter tone, "what the fuck are you doing?"

"Nothing, honest," Eric replied. "But she is prettier. And your nephew is a great guy. Don't worry, we will take care."

"There's more, Eric," Jon interrupted.

"Shit, what else could there be?"

"According to the cop, there is a plan for the Newark Police Chief to hold a press conference in the next couple of days identifying you and Bianca as co-conspirators in her husband's death. That's the kind of publicity that you don't need. So you need to wrap this up as soon as possible."

"They are having a press conference? Holy fucking shit!" he yelled, startling Leticia to the point where she almost drove onto the curb as she was pulling into the parking lot. "I can't have that!" He paused, and thought about his son finding out about why he was in Brazil. "Oh my God, Jason!"

"Calm down, man. I asked Fatima to tell Jason what was going on, not all of the details of course, but just the ones that he needed to know. I also told her to tell Bruce, so that he could deal with the family if things got out of hand. So they are taken care of."

"Thanks, I guess, but now I regret not telling Jason what was going on," Eric replied, rubbing his forehead with his free hand. "He is going to hate me for keeping this from him."

"No he won't," Jon interjected. "He will be proud of you for doing what you thought was right, and for trying to shield him from problems. That's good parenting, my friend. Perhaps you are finally learning something. And don't worry, I didn't tell Fatima about how Bianca blew you so neither Jason or Bruce will find out about that either."

Unfortunately for Eric, the last sentence was spoken at a volume loud enough for Leticia to hear. Eric looked over at her in horror, just in time to see a smile form on her face as she slowly nodded her head. "Oh, thanks for that, Jon. I will be careful here. If anything happens to me, either Steve or Leticia will call you. But I plan on being back to see you soon, at which time I am going to kick your ass for the last thing you said, because that it going to get me in trouble here." Leticia shook her head vigorously at the last comment.

"Goodbye, Uncle Jon," yelled Leticia, "we will come and visit you soon."

"Alright, you two, I am sorry to be the bearer of bad news," Jon said, "just please be careful. All of you be careful. I don't want anything to happen to any of you."

"Don't worry," Eric answered, "I will take care of them for you, and I will see you soon," he added, as he turned off the phone and waited for a snide comment from Leticia.

Leticia said nothing. She pulled into a parking space, turned off the engine, and opened the driver's side door. Exiting the car, she closed the door and, after Eric exited and closed his door, activated the car's alarm. Then she walked around the car, took Eric by the arm, and began to walk to the front door of the supermarket.

When they were about 20 feet from the entrance, however, she stopped, whirled, and smacked Eric in the left arm with her right hand. "I knew it," she yelled. Lowering her voice, she added, "and you are such a scumbag. Not for letting her give you *sexo oral*, but for lying to me."

"I know," he said, "but ..."

"No buts," she interrupted. "I want to trust you, and I want you to trust me. I have bared my soul to you," and then brought her voice to a whisper, "and I have bared my body to you also. And you lied to me."

"I am so sorry, Leticia, what can I do to make it up to you?" he pleaded. He stopped in the parking lot. "Really, I just didn't want you to think poorly of me. What can I do to make things right between us?"

She looked at him and smiled. "You're lucky that I am a nice person, Mr. Goldberg. Tell you what," she added, "I am going to let you squirm for a while. You will know later if I forgive you or not."

"I am confused," Eric answered, "how will I know?"

"Oh, you will know," she said. "trust me, you will know. But I am not going to tell you how. You will have to suffer for a while."

"If you say so," Eric said, dejectedly, "I deserve it." He suspected that it would have something to do with her manner of dress or levels of flirtation, but decided it was best to keep his thoughts to himself. "Now let's go into the market and get what we need so we can go back and plan for tonight."

"After you," Leticia said, motioning for Eric to walk into the store. As he stepped forward, she added, "and by the way, I already knew, you *cuzao*. Steve told me last night." Eric stopped walking. Leticia moved to her left, around him, and strode confidently into the store, followed by a sulking Eric.

"What exactly are we getting?" asked Eric, still sullen from Leticia's last comment but thinking that it would be best to change the topic as quickly as possible. "It would probably be faster if we split up and each picked up some of what we need."

"Good point," Leticia replied, "you go *para a esquerda* and I will go *para a direita*."

Eric looked at her, thought about what she had said for a moment, and then replied, "so you want me to go to the left and you are going to the right?"

"*Está certo!* (that's right!)," said Leticia, "see, you can be taught. Now, if you could only be taught to keep it in your pants, we would be all set…"

"Now, that hurt," Eric said, feigning mock pain. "Can't you let that drop for now?"

"For now, no, I don't think so. This one isn't going away that easily. Go to the left and get some fruit. Whatever you like, and get some bananas for Steve and a couple of mangoes for me. Then pick up some pasta, which is two aisles over, and I will get the rest. We will meet somewhere in the middle."

"You got it, boss," replied Eric. "See you back here in a little while." He walked to his left, to the far end of the store, and started picking fruit to bring back to the apartment.

Leticia went to the right, and walked over to where the fresh bread was sitting in various bins, arranged according to size and style. As she placed a few freshly-baked rolls into a bag, she stood next to a woman who was there with her two young daughters. The woman appeared to be about ten years older than her, and her hair was pulled back into a tight ponytail. *"Desculpe* (excuse me)," the woman said to Leticia, "do you mind if I reach in for a roll?"

"No problem," Leticia responded, "go ahead."

The other woman turned to the bigger girl. "Carla," she said, "how many rolls do you think we need?"

"I don't know, mommy," the girl replied, "how long are we staying with *tio Jose*?"

"For a while, I would think," the woman said. "Mommy needs to work things some things out. Let's just take eight. We can always come back if we need more."

The woman turned and, with her two girls, walked away, toward the next aisle. As she turned, Leticia could not help but notice her ample-sized chest. "Could it be?" she wondered to herself, "she spoke in English, and the girl spoke in perfect English. That's not normal for here." She took her rolls and ran to the other side of the store, trying to find Eric to see if she had, in fact, just been talking to Bianca Rodrigues.

She could not, however, locate Eric. He was not by the fruit, nor was he by the pasta. She looked up and down several aisles, finally locating him where she had started, by the bread. Breathless, she ran up to him, and told him that she thought that Bianca was in the same market. She grabbed him by the hand, and led him up and down the various aisles in what would prove to be a futile search for the mystery woman and her two daughters.

"I can't believe it," Leticia complained, "she was just here. How could she be gone so fast?"

"Do you really think it was her?"

"Yes, I do," answered Leticia.

"Why do you think that?" asked Eric.

"She spoke to me in English, and told one of her girls that they were staying with someone here until she worked some stuff out. The girl spoke perfect English. The kids down here learn it, Eric, but they certainly do not have perfect American accents like that girl had." Leticia paused to catch her breath, and raised her hands in front of her chest. "And when she turned to walk away," she added, "she had big *seios*, I mean breasts. I remembered what you said about them being bigger than mine, so I thought it could be her."

"Wait," said Eric, "you said that she had two girls with her. Did she call one of them by name?"

"I think so," Leticia replied, trying to remember if she had heard one of the girl's names. They walked up and down another couple of aisles, until Leticia stopped and grabbed Eric's arm. "Yes! She did call one of the girls by her name. She called the girl Carla."

Eric's face instantly turned pale, and he felt his knees start to buckle. "Holy shit," he said, "it was her. She's here. She is so fucking close." Now he began to run from aisle to aisle, with Leticia struggling to keep up. But there was no sign of Bianca Rodrigues in the market. He gave all of the groceries to Leticia and ran outside. He scanned the entire parking lot. Still, he saw no signs of Bianca Rodrigues.

He walked back into the store to help Leticia with the groceries. He was dejected that she had gotten away, but was, in a perverse way, pleased that she had been in the store with him. Now he knew for sure that she was in São Paulo, and, in all likelihood, she was staying with someone close by. His confidence grew that he would be able to find her for real. He still wondered, however, if he would be able to get her to confess to her crime. The plan had several levels to it. He could only accomplish some of them with Leticia and Steve's help. The rest would be up to his attempts at having Bianca tell the truth.

CHAPTER XXIII

Steve arrived home from work, as promised, a little after *meio-dia*. He found Leticia and Eric huddled over the kitchen table, which was covered with pages from that day's *Folha de S. Paulo*, the daily newspaper, as well as magazines trumpeting the nightly events taking place all over São Paulo. "Looks like you guys have been busy," Steve said as he walked into the kitchen, kissed Leticia, and, spying the open bottle of wine on the counter, reached into the cupboard, poured himself a glass and sat down. "What are you looking at?"

"We are trying to figure out the hot spots, where people will be going tonight and tomorrow night, to try to find a woman who, as we said last night, is trying to re-live her wild days as a *mulher solteira* (single woman)," explained Leticia. "And would you believe that she was in the store with us today?"

"You're joking," Steve replied. "How do you know?"

"I was buying rolls, and there was a woman next to me with two young girls. She was standing right next to me. She talked to me! She spoke to me in English, Steve," Leticia said, "and called her daughter Carla."

"I am pretty sure it was her, based on what Leticia told me," Eric added, "but I didn't see her. We ran through the whole store and into the parking lot, but by then she was gone." He paused. "Forget pretty sure. I am certain it was her. She apparently also said that she was staying with someone until she worked some stuff out, right Leticia?"

"That's right, I forgot that," added Leticia. "Plus, she had those big *seios*, just like Eric told me she had."

"*Seios*?" Steve asked. "Is that what you guys have been talking about? The size of women's tits? If that's the new way to identify people," he smiled, "then count me in."

"You can work on identifying me later," Leticia said as she sipped her own glass of wine, "and that's it for your police work, in case you are wondering."

"I figured," said Steve, dejectedly. "More importantly, what have you figured out for tonight?"

Leticia pointed to a half-page ad in the *Folha* which featured a young woman clad only in a string bikini. The ad contained that day's date, and a headline which blared, in big, bold letters, "*Noite das Muheres* (Ladies' night)." "I think that the best place to go is to *Vila Madalena*," Leticia responded, "that's where all of the best clubs are."

"Aren't there a bunch of gay bars there?" asked Steve. "I don't know why she would hang out in one of those."

Leticia looked at him disapprovingly. "You will have to excuse *meu namorado* (my boyfriend)," she said, shaking her head. "Apparently he is really *um homem velho chato* (a boring old man) who doesn't know what people his own age like to do. *Os jovens* (the young people) frequent the bars and clubs in the *Vila Madalena* section of São Paulo."

"Oh, they do?" Steve asked, curiously.

Leticia leaned in so that her breasts rested on the kitchen table. "Yes, they do," she said, in a seductive tone. "In fact, before I met boring old you, I used to go to the clubs there every week."

"Well excuse me," Steve said, "before I met you I would hang out in the *Bixiga* area. Sometimes, I would go to the *Vila Olimpia* neighborhood. There are clubs there too, you know."

"True," Leticia replied, reaching out with her left hand to stroke Steve's arm, "the *velho* is right. There are places in *Bixiga* and *Vila Olimpia,* which is really like a downtown where you find the biggest office buildings, sort of like mid-town Manhattan, I would say." She looked at Steve and smiled. "But if she really wants to enjoy herself, and she knows the area, she will be in *Vila Madalena.*"

"How far is this area from us?" Eric asked.

"Not far," Leticia replied. "It's over on the west side of the city. Without traffic ...," she laughed, "it would be about 15 minutes. So we should give ourselves a half hour to get there."

"*Bixiga* is closer to here," Steve interjected, "so it is certainly possible that she will be in *Bixiga.*"

"Let's do this," Eric intervened. "Let's go to *Vila Madalena* tonight, and then to *Bixiga* tomorrow if needed. Sound fair?" Both nodded their heads in agreement. "It's settled, then," he said, adding, "but that is not until late tonight. What should we do now?"

Leticia thought for a second. "I have an idea. She is here with her two girls, right? We need to find someplace for kids. They have only been here for a couple of days, so if we can pick out something that people would do with children while visiting here we may be able to find her."

"The park," Steve said. "That's where we should go."

"You mean *O Parque Ibirapuera?*" asked Leticia. "That's a great idea." Turning to Eric, she explained. "He's totally right. *Ibirapuera* park is a little to the west of us also, a little further south than *Bixiga*. We basically go the same way, but just need to go down the *Avenida Vinte e Tres de Maio* to get there, instead of the *Avenida Nove de Julho*. It's just like Central Park in New York. It is in the middle of the city, has museums, things to do for kids." Turning back to Steve, she added, "you are a *homem muito inteligente* (very smart man), *meu amor*."

"Sometimes," Steve replied, "but don't you forget it. Either of you." He stood and walked to the counter, returning with the bottle of wine as he poured everyone a fresh glass.

"The only question," pondered Leticia, "is where in the park they would go. If the girls are as young as I think they are, then they won't want to go to the *Museo de Arte Moderna* or *Museu do Folclore*." She rose to retrieve her laptop computer from the bedroom so that they could find the park's other attractions. After taking two steps, however, she stopped. "I know," she said, "the *planetário*, I mean, the planetarium!"

"I used to love the planetarium when I was a kid," Eric said.

"*Exatamente!*" Leticia exclaimed. "*Todas as crianças*, I mean, all children, love the planetarium. And with kids who just came here from the Northern Hemisphere, remember, it will be entirely different here, and even more interesting. That's where we should start today."

"Agreed," said Steve. "When do you want to leave?"

"As soon as possible," Leticia said. I need to change, of course. You should change also, get out of those work clothes. We may be chasing a woman today, you know, so you can't be wearing those old-man work shoes."

Eric looked up at Leticia. "I assume that I am dressed OK? I won't embarrass you?"

"You're fine, Eric," she replied. "Steve, go get changed. I will clean the kitchen and then get changed. It will only take me five minutes, I promise."

"Sounds like a plan," Steve said as he walked to the bedroom, loosening his tie as he closed the door behind him.

Leticia took the glasses and began to rinse them out, laying them on a towel next to the sink to dry. She took the now-empty wine bottle, rinsed it off, and laid it next to the glasses. Handing Eric a damp towel, she asked him to gather up the newspapers and other papers, and then to wipe down the table. He obliged, and then took the damp towel and hung it over the edge of the sink.

"Looks clean to me," Leticia said, "now let me go get changed." She walked toward her bedroom. As she was about five steps from the door, she stopped and removed her blouse. Turning to Eric so that he could see her breasts straining against the fabric of a pink lace bra, she added, "I must look like a mess." Turning back, she opened the door and entered her bedroom.

Eric smiled. Clearly that was the sign that she had forgiven him.

CHAPTER XXIV

"I know that it is really for kids, Eric, but you are going to love this planetarium," said Leticia as Steve drove the three of them to *Ibirapuera* Park. "We went there every year with school. It is shaped like a flying saucer, and shows the sky above San Paulo so it will be different from any one that you have been to in the United States."

"Sounds great," Eric replied. "When I was a kid, I used to love the planetarium. Astronomy was fun, learning about the Zodiac, constellations, stuff like that." He began to reminisce. "Everyone wanted to be an astronaut, right? Then you could explore new worlds, have freedom, not being stuck in the same space and same rut every day." He paused. "It's a shame, you know. You guys are still young. It's sad to be my age, look back, and wonder why you do something that you like only sometimes."

"What do you mean?" asked Leticia.

"Sometimes my job is great," Eric explained. "There are days when I go home, and I feel really good about what I have accomplished that day. But there are many days when I go home completely empty, like I have done nothing. It's not a good feeling." He turned to Steve. "Hopefully you really enjoy being an architect, and continue to enjoy it. I spend half of my time trying to figure out what I can do other than the law."

He paused and looked out the window, taking in some of the sights of São Paulo. "Actually, lately it's been much more often. Since the divorce, I have resented pretty much every day in that office. Most of my clients completely annoy me. My life has been shit, both in the office and at home. That's really no way to live."

"You need to live a little, Eric," Leticia replied. "Enjoy yourself more. If you do that, then everything else gets better."

"I know you are right. I look at you and how you seem to have so much fun living your life and I've been thinking that I should try to do the same. You know, sometimes I look up at the stars," Eric said, "and wonder what my life would have been like if I had become an astronaut. Looking up at stars gives me great peace, it gives me a sense that there are infinite possibilities for me, just like the sky itself is endless. That I am not destined to live the rest of my life in my office, chained to my desk with stupid clients."

"That's actually one of the bad things about living here in the city," Steve said. "There are so many buildings here, and so many lights, that it is like living in Manhattan, and you can't see the sky at night, so you can't see the stars. It's different from home. Plus, obviously, even if you could see the stars, they would be in a different layout than back home in either Jersey or Pennsylvania."

"It looks like I am going to the planetarium with two big boys of my own today," Leticia said, laughing. "Maybe I can even get you guys in for half-price, like the other children … oh, and one more thing, Eric," she said with obvious pride, "this is the first planetarium in the Southern Hemisphere, built in 1957, at least that is what they used to tell us."

"It's also nice how proud you are of your home, Leticia," Eric added, "it's been some time since I had pride like that for my home. It would be nice to be proud of something, or to be proud of myself again."

"You have much to be proud of, silly," Leticia replied. "You've just chosen to ignore those things. All that you need to do is search inside. They are there. Think about what makes you happy. Think about your son, Fatima, even Uncle Jon and your other friends. That's where your pride is based, and it is time to let it all out again."

Eric nodded in assent, and again looked out the window, this time comparing the landscape of São Paulo to that of his favorite areas of New Jersey, and the comparison was favorable.

As they turned on to the *Avenida Vinte e Tres de Maio*, Leticia told Steve that he would have to turn right and then likely need to go to the *Avenida Republica do Libano*, as the planetarium was closest to that roadway. The best way, she explained, was to turn onto the *Avenida Pedro Alvarez Cabral*. If there were parking lots along that road, then they could pull in there and walk to the planetarium. Otherwise, they would turn onto the *Avenida Republica do Libano* and pull into whatever entrance or parking lot they could locate.

The entrance was at the far end of the park, on the *Avenida Republica do Libano*. They pulled into the entrance, and Steve found the nearest lot. He parked the car and the three walked toward the planetarium, but were discouraged to find that it was not open. "*Merda!*" Leticia cried, reading the sign posted on the front doors. "I totally forgot. It is only open on weekends and holidays. We can't even get in there today."

"It's alright," Eric said, "let's walk around the park and see what else there is to do here. If we need to, we can always come back here on Saturday."

"I guess so, but I am still angry that I messed that up. I am really sorry." Leticia walked a few steps away from the planetarium, looking around in all directions as if trying to remember the other attractions at the park. "Let's try the *Pavilhao Japones*, the Japanese Pavilion," she suggested. "It's a big attraction in the park, and they have beautiful trees and buildings. It is perfect for young girls."

"Are you sure that it is open today?" asked Steve.

"Yes, it will be open. Even if the main building isn't open, we will still be able to walk around."

The three walked to the Japanese Pavilion. Eric paid the admission fee for them, and they walked around the gardens for the next hour. There were numerous families with young girls there as well, but there was no sign of Bianca Rodrigues. Leticia grew more exasperated by her mistake about the planetarium, and also was still annoyed at letting Bianca slip through her hands at the market. She was wracking her brain, trying to think of where else they could be in the park.

"One more idea," she said, "let's try the *Cicillo Matarazzo Pavilion*. I don't think that they will go to the museum there, but that is where they have the São Paulo Fashion Week every January and June. It was only a couple of weeks ago, and the area where they had the event should still have posters and stuff hanging up which show the models and fashions. If she is the way that you have described her, then I think she will want to take her children there and walk around."

The Pavilion was located on the other side of the park. It had been sunny, a perfect day for one to stroll along the park's walkways, but as they walked, the sky grew darker as clouds began moving above them. "Looks like rain," Eric said as he looked up.

"Probably," Leticia replied. "It rains here a lot. I don't know if you knew that. Sometimes it just rains for a few minutes and then clears up, just like it was when I lived in Miami."

"I did know that it rains here often," Eric said, quietly. "Someone told me that last week."

Leticia and Steve looked at each other, each of them realizing that Eric must have been referring to Bianca Rodrigues. They both nodded silently, agreeing that it would be best to allow the comment to pass without further elaboration.

When they arrived at the area where the Fashion Week festivities had been staged, they found several groups of people, mostly teenage girls, posing and vamping in front of the various posters and taking pictures of each other. There were a few families walking around in the area. At one point, Eric thought that he saw Bianca, but quickly realized that it was not her. Sitting on a park bench under the darkening sky, he began to feel Leticia's frustration.

"What am I doing here?" he asked aloud. "Do I really think that I can find someone in a city of millions of people? Who am I kidding?" He slumped forward, hanging his head as he tried to collect his thoughts. "It is impossible," he muttered to himself as he shook his lowered head slowly from side to side.

"No it isn't," said Leticia as she sat down next to Eric and placed her left hand over his shoulders. Pulling his head to her chest, she stroked his hair with her right hand and assured him that they would find Bianca Rodrigues, and that they would be able to find her over the next couple of days. "You can stay with us longer if you want, then, and really enjoy our city. Right, Steve?"

"Oh, of course," Steve chimed in. "Now both of you get up and let's try somewhere else. We should at least try to get inside before it starts to rain." He extended his hand to Eric, who pulled his head from its resting place on Leticia's ample chest and, reaching out, took Steve's hand and stood up. Leticia also stood, and the three searchers started to walk back to Steve's car, their mission at the park seemingly futile.

As they stood, they failed to notice the man sitting on the next bench. A young girl, who appeared to be five or six years old, sat with him. "*Tio Jose*," the young girl asked as the three adults walked past her, "where is mommy?"

Jose Neto looked down at the youngster and answered, "she will be right here, Leila. Stay here on the bench with me. She was just getting something from the car. I think she said her umbrella."

Raindrops began to fall as they made their way to the parking lot. They walked around the large lake in the middle of the park, its blue waters still shimmering despite the overcast sky. The skyline of São Paulo rose from behind the trees that ringed the lake's edges, its tall buildings rising majestically and some seemingly reaching the clouds which loomed ominously overhead. Choosing to ignore their dejection and failure of the day, Leticia was regaling Eric with facts about the city of São Paulo, and of

Brazil, so much so that he remarked that she could have a great career as a tour guide.

"But they wear such lousy outfits," Leticia said, "I could never wear them."

"Nice to know that we pass up work due to the clothes," Steve laughed, "do you see anything wrong with that, Eric?"

Before he could answer, Leticia grabbed Steve. "I don't have to work full-time now, though, because I have my big strong architect to work for both of us." She hugged him as forcefully as she had the night before, but this time he was able to maintain his balance. He swept her up so that her feet were off the ground, and walked to the water's edge.

"If you are not careful," he warned, "I am going to throw you into the lake." He made a shoving motion with his arms, and Leticia clung to him tighter as her body passed over the top of the water.

"Put me down," she ordered. "I don't want to get all wet."

"It's going to rain, anyway," said Eric, "so what is the difference?"

Leticia looked at Eric, her eyes widened in surprise. "Whose side are you on?" she shrieked. "Help me!"

Eric walked over to Steve. "Guess I have to act the chivalrous hero, young man." He extended his arms. "Give me the girl. Apparently she is ours now."

"No," Steve protested, smiling, "she's mine." By now Leticia was struggling to get free, and squirmed so much that Steve almost did drop her into the lake.

"She'll be wet in a couple of seconds the way she is squirming." Eric said, "give me the girl."

"You heard him," Leticia barked.

"Alright," Steve said, as he sighed deeply. "You guys are no fun. You can have her." He heaved Leticia slightly upward, and then planted her into Eric's waiting arms, her arms immediately wrapping around Eric's neck for safety.

"My hero," Leticia exclaimed as she tightened her grip around Eric's neck and gently kissed his cheek. "Don't ever put me down," she added, looking back at Steve, "this is the safest I have ever felt."

"If you say so," Eric replied, "but don't forget how old I am. I am going to drop you any minute," he said as he started to lose his left hand's grip, the one that was tucked underneath her bent knees. Struggling to maintain his grip and balance, he reached under her and his hand found its way to her ass, where it remained until he was steady on his feet.

"Happy now?" she whispered as his hand enveloped her right cheek, "good thing I wasn't wearing a skirt or you'd really have your hand on my ass." He quickly moved his hand back to underneath her knees, before Steve was able to realize what had happened.

"I'm going to put you down now," Eric said, "before I drop you." He lowered his left hand so that her legs and feet went down to the ground. She maintained her grip around his neck, though, so that when he let her go they were standing toe-to-toe, with his neck locked in her embrace.

"Jealous, Steve?" she laughed, as she rested her head on Eric's shoulder.

"I would think not," Steve replied, "good luck with her, Eric. You're going to need it."

"You're giving up on me that easily?" Leticia asked, her voice muffled as her face pressed against Eric's shoulder.

"*Naturalmente, meu amor*," he replied, and all three of them shared a laugh.

Leticia raised her head and went to kiss Eric on the cheek for saving her from being dropped into the lake. As she looked forward, however, she froze. Her grip around Eric's neck grew tighter.

"Uh, Leticia," Eric gasped, "you're hurting me a little."

"Shhh," she replied.

"What do you mean, shhh? I can't breathe here."

"She's here," Leticia whispered in his ear. "I can see her with the girl. It's the same girl from yesterday. Shut up so that she doesn't hear your voice."

Now it was Eric who froze as drops of rain started to fall faster and harder from the cloud-covered sky. "How close is she?"

"Almost close enough for us to reach her if she tries to run. They're both wearing sneakers. If we move too soon, they will be gone. Just keep holding me for now, so she won't realize we are looking for her."

They were whispering so low that Steve could not hear their conversation, which would prove to be a problem. "Jesus, guys," he cried, "can you please stop this crap so we can get moving? I've had enough of this love-fest. I don't want to be out here in the rain, and we need to look for …" At that moment he looked to his right and saw the woman with her daughter walking toward them. She had long, wavy hair, looked to be in her mid-thirties, and had, as Eric had described it, a large chest. "Holy shit!" he cried, "is that her over there?"

"Quiet, you idiot," Leticia admonished him, "we know. That's why we are standing so still." But it was too late. Bianca Rodrigues also heard Steve's cry. Looking at the trio of people standing only thirty yards or so away from her, she saw the face of a young woman next to the back of a man's head. She thought that the man's head looked somewhat familiar.

In an instant, it became clear. "Eric?" she mouthed silently. "It can't be." She stopped dead in her tracks, holding her daughter's hand tightly so that she did not move forward either.

"Is something wrong, mommy?" the girl asked. She tried to take a step forward, but her mother's tight grip pulled her back.

"No, *bebê*, everything is fine. Just stand here for a second. I want to see something."

The man who was facing her started to walk toward her, and Bianca took a step backward, a step which her daughter emulated. The young woman kept staring at her, and slowly released the other man from her grip. He slowly turned to the side, and Bianca was now sure – "shit," she thought to herself, "it's Eric! *Como diabos ele chegou aqui? (*How the fuck did he get here?) If he knows about the note to the police, he's going to try something." Clearly, she knew, he was there for her. "*Vamos,* Carla," she said quietly, "fast. Don't ask me why. Let's just go."

Bianca watched as the other man starting to sprint toward them. As he did, Bianca turned, grabbed Carla's hand, and started to run away. The rain intensified as they ran through the park. Leaving the concrete walkways, Bianca led her daughter through the tree-lined paths, their sneakers sloshing through the mud puddles that were forming from the now heavy rain. They took various turns through the wooded areas, leaving the paths in order to escape. Minutes later, when it became apparent that they had lost their pursuers, they ducked into the nearest building.

Bianca frantically called Jose Neto on his cell phone. "*Ele está aqui, Jose. He is here,*" she said, breathlessly. "*Eu não sei como, mas ele está aqui no parque* (I don't know how, but he is here in the park). We need to get out of here, now!" She turned and looked in all directions to make sure that none of her pursuers had located her position. "Go to the car with Leila and pull it out of the lot. Drive north to the edge of the park and then turn right. I will walk out of the trail there and you can pick us up. They can't find me again."

Although she never called him by name, Jose suspected that she was talking about Eric Goldberg. The urgency in her voice was greater than ever before, even when they were plotting the demise of Joao Rodrigues. He scooped Leila Rodrigues up in his arms, and ran to the car so that he could meet Bianca.

At the same time, an exhausted and drenched Eric Goldberg stood, hunched over, on one of the paths that wound its way through the *Ibirapuera* Park. Both Steve and Leticia were well ahead of him, but he could hear them calling to each other that they had lost Bianca Rodrigues. "I can't believe this," Leticia called to both Steve and Eric, "this is the second time. I can't believe this."

They both walked slowly back to where Eric was standing. Steve was drenched, his hair matted down, and he was cursing himself for letting a woman and her young child run faster than he could. His legs were splattered with mud as a testament to his running through the mud-laced pathways, and his calves ached because it was the first time that he had run in as long as he could remember.

Leticia was also very wet from the rain, her long, way hair straightened by its dampness and her lightly-colored t-shirt turned translucent. The pink color of her bra shone through the wet t-shirt like a beacon, and her breasts heaved as she gasped for air.

"Let's go," she croaked, her words barely audible through her heavy breaths. "Let's go back to the car." The others nodded in agreement, and the three of them walked back to the parking lot in silence. As they approached Steve's car, none of them noticed the blue car speeding out of the lot, nor did they know that its driver, Jose Neto, was on his way to pick up their quarry. Within minutes, Bianca Rodrigues would be safely inside of Jose's car, being whisked back to his apartment and out of their reach.

Steve unlocked the car doors, and then went to the back of the car and fished two towels out of the trunk. He threw one to Eric, and handed one to Leticia. "Here," he told them, "use this to dry off a little." Steve ran his hands through his hair to release some of the water that had adhered to his hair and scalp, and quickly wiped off his arms and muddy legs as the rain continued to come down. Eric took his towel and wiped off the top of his head, and then used it to wipe off his arms and legs before entering the rear seat. Leticia toweled off her long hair as best as possible, and then wiped down her arms and legs as well before ducking into the front passenger's seat.

Once inside the car, however, the occupants' discomfort increased as their wet clothes began to adhere to their bodies. In response, both Steve and Eric peeled off their shirts, throwing them in a heap onto the floor alongside Eric. Leticia then followed suit, taking off her soaked shirt and tossing it back to Eric to put on the floor.

"Jesus, Leticia," Steve cried, "what are you doing?"

Leticia, sitting in her pink bra and shorts and attempting to dry her neck and chest with the towel, snapped back quickly. "*Relaxe, idiota*, I am putting the towel around me." She wrapped the towel around her torso, so that only the pink straps of her bra protruded from atop the towel. "Besides," she began to yell, "Mr. Goldberg here is in his 40's. He was married. And as we all now know, a few days ago he got *sexo oral* from the fucking woman that we are chasing. *Tenho certeza que já viu mulheres em sutiãs antes!* (I am sure that he has seen women in bras before)!"

"But he hasn't seen you in a bra!" Steve yelled, "or has he?"

Even in her anger, Leticia knew when to draw the line. "No," she said quietly. "But you know what," she said, again raising her voice, "be glad that the bra is still on," she barked, as she snapped one of its straps against her shoulder. "You have no idea how *desconfortável (*uncomfortable) I am right now."

"Why the fuck are you so mad at me?" Steve demanded. "I didn't make it rain."

"*Por que eu estou com raiva de você?* Why am I mad at you, is that your question?" yelled Leticia. "I will tell you why. Why couldn't you keep your mouth shut?" She pointed her index finger and wagged it in Steve's direction. "If you hadn't said anything, you loudmouth, she would have come closer and we could have gotten her. *Eu já tinha visto ela.* I had already seen her. I had told Eric. We knew she was there." Now she was shrieking. "We knew she was there! Do you hear me? *Nós sabíamos que ela estava lá!* If you had just kept your mouth shut this wouldn't have happened."

"You've got to be kidding me!" Steve shot back. "How was I supposed to know that you saw her? As best as I knew, you were just flirting with Eric. That's the sight that I am used to by now." His face turned a deep red with anger, and veins bulged from his forehead and neck as he yelled. "Maybe if you weren't so busy hugging and kissing him, and leading him on like a cheap whore, you would have been able to tell me that you knew that she was there. And while we are talking about her, you let her go yesterday!"

"Is that what you think of me?" Bianca asked in a hurt voice, "that I am a *prostituta?*" She raised her hand as if to slap Steve, but stopped short as she began to cry. "I can't believe this. *Você sabe o quanto eu te amo.* You know how much I love you. I just like to have fun. You knew that about me when you met me," she added, burying her head in her hands as she sobbed.

The raindrops and Leticia's sobbing formed the only sounds in the car. Those sounds were soon joined by the deep sign which emitted from Steve's throat. "Fuck," Steve said, exasperated, as his face turned a more normal color. "I know you love me, and I love you too. I just wish you turned it down a notch once in a while." He reached out and took her hand from her face, as tears continued to stream down her face. "I am still getting used to this whole 'Brazilian girl' thing." He pulled her closer to him and hugged her over the gearshift, causing her towel to come unbundled and drop to the seat. Steve looked down at her bra-covered chest, shrugged his shoulders, smiled, and said, "Maybe I could get used to this." Leticia smiled, and kissed him.

"Guys, guys," Eric said as Leticia sat back in her seat, again lifting the towel to cover herself, "maybe I could get used to it also, but you have got to stop fighting. Nobody is at fault. We are all doing what we think is best." He put his hands on the backs of the front seats and pulled himself forward so his head was between theirs. "I have heard enough fighting, and enough yelling. You're happy now, but I don't want to hear you guys accusing each other anymore." He took a deep breath. "You are both doing me a big favor by trying, and I really appreciate all that you have done. We didn't get her. I am discouraged also. But we will have to try again. And if we don't get her, it should not cause any friction between you. That is not my intent, and I will feel worse if you guys fight over this. So stop it. Let's go home and re-tool."

"But we are OK, now," Steve said, "right, baby?"

"Yes we are," Leticia replied as she took his hand, "maybe better than OK. I think we are all learning a little bit about ourselves and each other today."

Steve nodded, and an unsettling silence fell over the car. Eric sat back, his bare back against the car seat and damp towel. He sighed and looked out the window at the rain, which had gotten stronger and was now pelting the vehicle. Steve also sighed, and looked over at his girlfriend, still a vision of loveliness even with her makeup all messy and hair all knotted from the rain. "He is right. I am sorry, *querida*. No more yelling, OK?"

"*Claro, meu amor*. Let's work together. I am just so frustrated, and most of it is really aimed at me. I was wrong to yell at you. Let's go home, get cleaned up, and see what we can do later."

"Sounds good, guys, let's go," chimed in Eric. He was pleased that they had stopped fighting and had theoretically made up until the next explosion but was more worried than ever now about his ability to catch Bianca Rodrigues. She knew that he was in São Paulo. His ability to sneak up on her had passed. Perhaps having three people on the hunt was simply too unwieldy. But he needed their help. He closed his eyes, trying desperately to determine the best way to find her again.

"Eric?" called Leticia from the front seat.

"Yes?" he replied, opening his eyes.

"I'm so sorry," she said, as she again began to cry, her tears mixing with whatever old tears and raindrops still remained on her face. She lifted the towel to dry her face, hiding beneath the cloth as her body wracked with sobs.

"Don't be," Eric said, trying to comfort Leticia, "and please don't cry. Take your head back out of there," he instructed, and she lifted her head, wiped her face one more time with the towel, and then let the towel drop, again revealing her bra, as she turned back to Eric.

Leticia took a few short breaths in an attempt to calm herself, and then lifted her hand and reached back to Eric. "Really," she croaked, "I am so sorry."

Eric took her hand and kissed it, holding it against his cheek for a couple of seconds. "It will work out," he said, "I know it will work out." He thought that he convinced her, but he was still having trouble convincing himself.

CHAPTER XXV

Back at the apartment, the two men sat on the couch and drank wine while Leticia showered. "Unbelievable," Steve said, "we had her so close. What are the odds?"

"That's why I am a little worried about the odds on seeing her again," Eric replied, "but please do not say anything to Leticia. She is taking this very hard, and I don't want you to have any problems because of me."

Steve stood and walked into the kitchen to pull some crackers out of the cabinet and two bricks of cheese from the refrigerator. "Don't worry about her," he said as he walked away. "She will be fine. She's tough, believe me. She's really competitive, especially internally. She pushes herself very hard." He looked to make sure that she was still in the shower. "And that stuff from before wasn't really about you. It has been brewing for some time. We need to work some stuff out. But ironically, I think that the explosion today has taken us in the right path, so I owe you thanks."

"My pleasure, I guess, and no doubt," Eric called to him in response. "But still, I don't want there to be extra friction between you two. There's no reason for it, and you certainly don't need it."

Steve re-emerged, placed the cheese and a knife on a board in the center of the table, and opened the box of crackers and spilled some onto the board alongside the cheese. "I appreciate that, but you shouldn't worry about us. We need to worry about you. What do you think we should do tonight?" he asked.

"I think we have to go out and look for her in the club tonight, for two reasons," Eric replied. "First, if the US feds do actually contact the local police here, then it will be harder for me to go out with every passing day."

"Understood," said Steve.

"And second, at least for tonight, she will feel empowered."

"Who will feel empowered?" asked Leticia, as she emerged from her bedroom, wearing only her Penn State t-shirt and a towel wrapped around her still-wet hair. "Bianca?"

"Yes, Bianca," answered Eric. "I think she will feel strong today, that we had her and blew it, and that she will want to go out tonight and celebrate. Once her false euphoria wears off tomorrow it will be different. So tonight is our chance."

"Sounds right to me," said Leticia, as she took a glass from the cupboard and poured some wine. She placed the glass on the table and took a piece of cheese before sitting on the chair alongside the couch. She sat cross-legged, and her light green underwear peeked out from beneath her dark, navy-colored T-shirt. "The only question is where she will go. Are we still planning on going to *Vila Madalena* tonight?"

"From what you have told me, I would think that that sounds like the best idea," Eric replied. "Why don't we head down that way for dinner, and then we can hit a club or two. That should increase our chances."

"We should leave in a couple of hours. I am going to take a quick nap to rest up for later. Steve, entertain Eric. See you boys in a little while." She took her glass of wine and retreated to her bedroom, closing the door behind her so that she would not be disturbed by the sounds of Steve and Eric speaking to each other.

"If it weren't raining I would say that we could go check out one of the stadiums," Steve said. "Leticia told me that you asked about them. I have to confess that I still don't really follow the local soccer, so I don't even know if they are playing now. In fact," he explained, "that is one of the big issues that she has with me, if you haven't noticed. She's all mad about the fact that I haven't taken enough interest in Brazil and its culture. In fact, that's why she told me you asked about the stadiums. Not to make you feel badly, but she gave me hell over it because you asked on the car ride back from the airport and I still have never asked her about it."

"Oh, shit, man," Eric replied, "I am so sorry."

"Don't be," Steve said as he raised the glass to his lips. "I deserved it. Maybe your being here is a little wakeup call for me to pay more attention not just to her, but also to her background and culture." He sat back, pondering his epiphany. "Maybe if it clears up tomorrow we can check one out, but let's see if there is a game on television now." He reached into a pouch on the side of the couch and pulled out a remote control, pushed a button, and the television came on. He scrolled down a few channels, and the images of a soccer game came on. It was actually highlights from the past week's events, but Eric asked if they could watch, wanting to experience whatever form of Brazilian soccer as he could while he was in the country. "Sure," Steve said, "Leticia would appreciate your efforts."

"You know what, Steve," Eric said as the men watched the highlights and strained to listen to the Portuguese-language commentary, "maybe this is a wake-up call for all of us. I was just going through the motions at work and at home. The threat of losing everything, though, makes me want to keep it more. Maybe I needed this, in a twisted sort of way."

Ironically, however, despite the fact that he was experiencing what he termed a "wake-up call," the day's events took their toll on Eric and he was asleep, on the couch, within ten minutes. Steve turned the volume on the television down, and walked into his bedroom, figuring he was better off napping with Leticia than he would be with Eric. He would take the time to learn about soccer, he thought to himself, but for now he wanted to be next to Leticia. His learning process could wait, until such time as he could watch the games with Leticia and she could explain them to him, and could certainly wait until after their mission was completed and Bianca Rodrigues was brought to justice.

Two hours later, Eric was awakened by the sound of heels clicking on the hallway's floors. As he struggled to open his eyes, a fully-dressed and perfectly made-up Leticia Alves walked over to the couch, leaned over, and gently put her hand on his shoulder to make sure that he was awake. "Wake up, *dorminhoco* (sleepy-head)," she purred. "It's time for you to get dressed."

"I'm awake," he groaned, "I just can't open my eyes."

"Try harder," she answered, "you may like what you see."

He opened his eyes and adjusted to the light in the room. Before him stood Leticia, resplendent in a bright blue dress, with a neckline that plunged down below her cleavage and with a bottom hem that rested just above her knees. The gap between her breasts was accented by a white gold chain, from which a heart-shaped charm dangled precariously, and by a single band of steel-colored fabric which held the sides of the dress together and which would presumably keep her breasts from escaping, even during a vigorous round of dancing. In her hand she carried shoes with heels that were at least five inches high, which meant that when she laced them around her feet, she would be taller than both him and Steve. Her hair looked wavier than usual, and fell over her shoulders in what appeared to be a perfect circle pattern. "So," she asked, "what do you think?"

He sat on the edge of the couch and rubbed his eyes before standing. "You look *bela*, Leticia. Absolutely *bela*." He leaned in and kissed her on both cheeks, causing her to blush. "Now let me go and get dressed, but I fear that it will be nowhere as much an event as you in that dress."

"You don't want to be an event, *meu amor*," she cautioned him. "You want to blend, and not be noticed. She won't recognize me. She saw me once, in the rain. She knows what you look like. In fact, as we both know, she knows what most of your body looks like," she added, winking. "You need to be invisible."

CHAPTER XXVI

The futile search for Bianca Rodrigues continued through the night. There was no sight of her at the restaurant where her three pursuers ate dinner, nor did she appear at either of the clubs where they went afterward. Far from being invisible, as he had been told to be by Leticia, Eric was conspicuous at each dancing venue, as he stood, sullen, on the side of the dance floor and scanned the assembled crowd from side to side, looking to everyone else like a policeman searching for illegal activity.

Leticia and Steve had tried to work through the clubs, dancing at intervals and mingling through the crowds to get a full perspective of those dancing, but who may not have been visible from Eric's vantage point on the sidelines. Though it was not their intent, they found the dancing an enticing and exhilarating diversion. At the second club, moreover, Leticia had had seen enough of Eric's sulking and stalking the sidelines. She went up to Eric, extended her hand, and asked, "*você dança comigo, senhor*? (will you dance with me, sir?)"

Eric, understanding the words "*dança*" and "*comigo*" to mean "dance with me", politely declined. But Leticia would not take no for an answer. Slithering up to him and lightly gyrating her hips as she wrapped her arms around his neck, she demanded, "*dança comigo, senhor. Agora!* (dance with me, sir. Now!)" Finally, Eric capitulated. Leticia took him by the hand and led him to the middle of the dance floor. There, amidst the pulsating beat of the music, he was able to forget about Bianca Rodrigues and the Newark Police Department. He was able to just dance, to just enjoy Leticia's company, and to enjoy watching those around him enjoy their own dancing.

It was the first time that he truly felt liberated since he first read about Joao Rodrigues' death, the first time that he had allowed himself to enjoy life in months, and, while it was temporary, it was a welcome respite from his obsessive quest to find Bianca Rodrigues and bring her to justice. The two were later joined by Steve, who proudly showed off some dance moves that he had learned since moving to Brazil. Minutes melted into hours, and before they knew it the clock had struck 2:00 AM. The dance floor was still packed at that time and the crowd was showing no signs of thinning, but when they realized the late hour all three agreed that it was time for them to leave and get some sleep before reconvening to begin their quest anew the next morning.

Unlike the afternoon, the fact that they had not apprehended Bianca did not weigh heavily on them; to the contrary, they had, in essence, recharged their batteries so that they were completely ready for tomorrow's attempt. They each felt a different form of refreshment – for Leticia and Steve, a rejuvenation of their romance and, also for Steve, a recognition of the new culture in which he had immersed himself. For Eric, it was the understanding that he could enjoy himself again and love himself again, and that his sulking in Brazil while chasing after Bianca Rodrigues was not that much different than the sulking that he had been doing, on a daily basis, since the implosion of his marriage.

The thumping of the music and the all-but-forgotten feelings of liberation and happiness still resonated through Eric's head as they drove home. The same was true for the noises of raindrops striking the car's exterior, which provided a rhythmic soundtrack to the journey. Leticia dozed in the front passenger's seat as Steve negotiated the streets in between *Vila Maladena* and their neighborhood. Eric was just starting to think about what they should do the next day when Steve spoke. "I was a little surprised that we didn't see her tonight," he said, "what you said before made sense to me."

"Well, then," Eric replied, "I have been thinking about this. Maybe, maybe we should be thinking just the opposite. If she knows that I am here and looking for her, maybe she thinks that the police are here looking for her also. And if she thinks that, …"

"Then she would keep a low profile," Steve said, finishing Eric's thought.

"Exactly. Now, if she thinks that the police here are looking for her, what will she do?"

"Well," said Steve, "I guess if she is staying with someone other than family, she can hide out in that home until she thinks that the police aren't looking for her anymore."

"True," pondered Eric, "but wouldn't it make more sense to get away until the heat is off?" He smacked the seat with his right hand, its noise waking Leticia. "That's it!"

"What's it?" Leticia mumbled as she continued to rest her head against the seat, her eyes still closed.

"She's going to leave São Paulo! She probably went home today after we saw her and booked a flight out somewhere, like to Brasilia, because Rio, if my geography is correct, is even too close. She will take her girls with her, and since she does not want to alarm them too much, she couldn't leave today, so that it does not seem too rushed to them."

"So when, tomorrow?" asked Steve.

"If I had to make a bet," Eric replied, "yes, she will be leaving tomorrow morning. We need to get up early tomorrow and get to the airport."

"But which one?" mumbled Leticia, "don't forget, there are a few airports here."

"I do know, but when I was looking to book a flight here I was instructed to fly into the one named after the Governor, GRU," Eric replied. "That's also the closest to you, I think, and if she is staying near you guys then that is the most logical choice. That's where we need to go."

"Then it is settled," Steve said, "GRU it is. How early do we leave?"

"Let's think about that also," replied Eric. "She has the girls with her, so she won't want to leave too early. Tomorrow is Saturday, so traffic won't be as bad as during the week, I hope. Figure she will have a 9:00 or so flight, so we should leave around 6:00 or so to try to beat her there. If it is still raining, also, it might take a little longer to get there. So, yes, 6:00 will be best, I think."

"Let's hope it stops raining before then," Leticia added, "or else we may have a problem with the *Marginal Tiete*. In big rains, it sometimes floods at parts, and that is the easiest way to get back to the airport."

"So 6:00 it is. And it may be our last chance," Eric said, "so I hope it goes our way."

CHAPTER XXVII

"A lawyer may reveal [confidential client] information to the extent the lawyer reasonably believes necessary ... to rectify the consequences of a client's criminal, illegal or fraudulent act in the furtherance of which the lawyer's services had been used."

- New Jersey Rules of Professional Conduct Paragraph 1.6(c)(1)

Eric's watch read 6:15. He and Steve stood, waiting, in the living room of the apartment while Leticia finished getting dressed. The rain outside continued, as it had through the night, and they had already heard reports on the radio about possible flooding throughout the city. He started to pace, nervously, as Steve beckoned to Leticia to hurry up. "It's only 6:15," she called from behind the closed bedroom door. "There's still plenty of time."

"I apologize for her," Steve said to Eric. "She is normally late. We should have told her 5:30. Then we would have had at least a chance of leaving on time."

"Don't worry, it is fine," Eric replied, although he was growing slightly disconcerted about the delay.

Leticia opened the bedroom door, at which point Steve tried to usher her directly out of the apartment. "Just a second," she cried, "don't rush me. We will get there." She walked into the kitchen, opened the refrigerator, and pulled out some fruit for the three of them to eat in the car on the way to the airport. "One would think that you guys could have taken care of this, since you were waiting for me," she added, condescendingly.

"One might, but then one would be wrong," Steve replied, "now let's go." He led her to the apartment door, escorted her through, and then closed and locked the door after Eric exited. They walked to the car, and this time Eric sat in the front passenger's seat while Leticia went to the back, where she could stretch out, eat her fruit, and then sleep during the drive. The rain had intensified, and already some of the local streets seemed impassable. Steve maneuvered his way through the neighborhood with the deft skill of a Formula 1 driver, however, and soon they found themselves on the *Marginal Tiete* en route to the airport.

Leticia pulled a knife from her pocketbook and began to cut pieces of a mango that she had taken from the refrigerator. As she ate, she offered pieces to both of the men, each of whom politely refused. Luckily, the traffic on the highway was fairly light, testament to the rains, and Steve drove at such a speed, seemingly unaffected by the rain, that he would periodically catch up to and then pass small groups of cars. Leticia cut a slice of the fruit as Steve approached the next such cluster. Looking to the right as he passed a sequence of cars in the next lane, she saw a blue car alongside them; a man was driving, and there were two young girls in the back seat.

Leticia did a double-take when she saw the girl seated behind the driver. "Oh my God, Eric," she yelled, "there's the girl in the blue car next to us. Don't pass it, Steve, that's the daughter."

"Are you serious?" Eric asked, squinting so he could see inside the car, his vision partially obscured by the raindrops on the windows of each car. He did not recognize the driver, but in the passenger seat, hair hidden under a baseball cap and wearing large sunglasses despite the fact that they were driving in a rainstorm, sat Bianca Rodrigues. "Shit, that is her," he yelled, "They're in the next car!"

"What should I do?" yelled Steve. "We're going about 50 now, and it's a little slippery out there. I should just pace them for now?"

"Should we signal them?" asked Leticia, "like ask him to pull over?"

"I don't think so," Eric replied. "I don't think he will be overly compliant, and if we can just pace him like this we can get her when they come to a stop, whether at the airport or not." He turned forward so that the driver would not see him staring into the car.

Leticia, however, kept her eyes directly on the blue car and its occupants. "Uh oh," she squealed, "we have a problem. She saw you!" Leticia saw Bianca Rodrigues turn to the left, and all of a sudden her mouth opened wide as if she was screaming and she started to point at Eric. She and the driver were speaking furiously, and she seemed to be motioning for the driver to turn into the car, as if to run them off of the road.

"We have another problem," Steve yelled, "I am seeing signs that the road is flooded up ahead. We're going to have to get off soon, and we may lose them then."

"Just try to stay with them," Eric pleaded. "Give me a couple of minutes and I will figure out what we should do."

Jose Neto, however, acting on the instructions of his girlfriend, had no intention of providing Eric with any time to gather his thoughts. All of a sudden, he turned the wheel of his car sharply to the left, and the front of his car rammed into the passenger's side door of Steve's car, directly where Eric was sitting. "Holy shit!" Steve cried as he struggled to steady the car, "doesn't that asshole know that he will kill us all?"

"It looks like the flooded part of the road is closer than we thought," Eric yelled, pointing to the roadway which lay in front of the car. "It's right there. Turn to the right, into their car. This is our chance!"

Steve jerked the wheel to the right, catapulting the car into the next lane. Anticipating the move, Jose Neto had sped up, so that the front of Steve's car did not strike the front side of his car, but rather the impact was with the rear door on the driver's side. The strength of the impact, however, forced Jose's car into a spin, and, when it caught the additional rainwater up ahead, the car fishtailed over the edge of the paved part of the roadway and came to rest off to the side of the road, its front smashing against a retaining wall barrier, where it sat, idling, in a foot of water from the flooding river.

Steve pulled his car over to the side of the road, and he and Eric rushed from the car and ran to Jose's car as fast as he could, sloshing through the flood waters. Neither of the doors on the driver's side of the vehicle was operational, and Jose lay slumped, unconscious, over the steering wheel, the heavy fabric of his air bag separating him from the wheel itself. Both girls were in the back, crying. Bianca also lay in the front seat, the deployed air bag crumpled in her lap. Eric could not tell if she was conscious, but could see that she was breathing as her chest sporadically moved up and down.

He ran to the passenger's side of the car, and, seeing that the rear door was locked, implored Leila Rodrigues to open the door. Initially she was afraid to even touch the door, but soon agreed and was able to push the door open. Eric lifted her out of the car and carried her to Steve's vehicle, where Leticia waited. The young girl appeared to have no injuries, and appeared to be crying due to her fright from the multiple impacts, and not from any physical pain. In the meantime, Steve climbed into the back seat, reached across, and helped Carla Rodrigues out into the rain. She had suffered some small cuts to her face and left arm when the window to her door shattered in the impact with Steve's car, and Steve carried her to the car, handed her to Leticia, and then pulled a first aid kit from his trunk so that Leticia could tend to her wounds.

While Steve and Leticia were caring for Carla, Eric walked back to the passenger's side of Jose's car and opened the front door. Bianca's head lay back against the headrest of the seat, bruises burned into the outside of her eyes where the airbag had impacted with her sunglasses. Her lip was cut, and there was a cut on her cheek. Her eyes were closed. He reached out and touched her right shoulder, which caused her to flinch in pain. He determined that she must have injured the shoulder by slamming it against the door during one of the vehicle-to-vehicle impacts.

He again reached out to her, this time on her right leg. "Bianca," he said, "you need to wake up. Are you OK?"

She stirred, making a moaning sound before responding. "*Meu ombro dói (*My shoulder hurts)."

"*No falo portugues,*" he responded, "can you tell me in English?"

"My shoulder hurts," she mumbled. "Why don't you speak Portuguese?"

"Bianca, it's me, Eric. Eric Goldberg."

She opened her eyes, attempting to focus. "My eyes hurt a lot too," she said. "I can't see anything."

"You got some bruises from the airbag hitting your glasses. But you can open them. Try again."

She again struggled to open her eyes and slowly fixed her gaze on Eric's face. "Eric," she said, looking around, "what are you doing here? What happened?"

"Why I am here is not important right now," he replied. "You were in an accident. Your boyfriend was driving and tried to ram another car."

"Oh," she said, "my boyfriend." Suddenly her eyes opened wide. "My boyfriend!" she shouted, "Jose, is he ok?" The facts of the accident seemed to be returning to her memory. "*Meu Deus!* (Oh my God!)" she shrieked, "meus bebês. O que aconteceu com meus bebês? (my babies, what happened to my babies?)"

"The girls are fine and in my car, if that is what you just asked me," Eric replied. "Carla has a few cuts but my friend already bandaged them up, and Leila is fine."

"I need to see them," she shrieked, but when she tried to stand the pain in her shoulder, and now her right side, proved to be too great as she slumped back down in the sear. "I need to see my babies," she cried.

"I will bring them over in a minute," Eric said, "but first, we have something to discuss." Sirens began to blare in the distance. Eric knew that he had to make her agree to tell the police the truth before they arrived, or else they would whisk her away to a hospital before his name would be cleared. "We need to talk about your letter to the Newark police."

"Letter, what letter to the police?" Bianca moaned.

"You know what I am talking about," he barked. "You almost ruined my life, you know."

"Yes, I guess I did." She started to cry. "I don't know what I was thinking," she whispered between sobs. "Look at this mess. I was with Jose, and Joao was such a bad person to me. I didn't know what else to do. It may not make things better, but you've never been in a situation like that so you wouldn't understand."

"You would be surprised," he answered. "I have been in such horrible situations. Up until recently, life itself was a terrible situation for me. But I would never do what you did, or do anything like it."

"Really?" she asked, in a weak voice. "I thought that I had to do it."

"Well, I know what you have to do now. You have to tell the police that I had nothing to do with killing your husband."

"I do?" she asked, wearily.

"Yes," he said, grabbing her face by the jaw and pulling it toward him as she winced in pain. "You need to clear this up now, so I can go home. I don't care if you stay here and the government here doesn't extradite you back to the U.S., but I need my name cleared. *Me entende?*"

"Yes, I understand," she answered. "I am sorry for all of this, Eric. But I did it for my children. I had to. You're a father, you understand."

"I understand lots of things, Bianca," Eric answered. "But trying to send someone else to jail and ruining their life? That is just plain wrong, even if it was a lousy life. As I said before, I wouldn't do that to anyone. That I do not understand. And to tell you the truth, in the last couple of days, I have learned that I have to start enjoying life again. I want it. I want to enjoy it, and to live it." He leaned in as the sirens grew nearer. "And I am not going to let you take that away from me, no matter what you say or offer to me." His voice lowered to a growl as he again grabbed her by the face, her eyes opening widely as pain shot through her body. "Now, are you going to tell the police?"

Bianca sighed deeply and choked back more tears. "Yes," she replied, "I will tell the police. You're right. You should be able to enjoy your life. They may never even turn me over to Newark so me and the girls can just stay here with Jose. Now please let go of my face, you are really hurting me." She looked to her left. "He's breathing, right?"

Eric looked over to Jose. "Yes he is, and the police and paramedics will be here to take care of him."

"I was right the first time, you know," Bianca said. "You really are a nice guy. I never should have done this to you." She looked up at him, tears in her eyes. "Can you please hold my hand until the police get here? It would make me feel much better," she asked, raising her left arm across her chest.

Eric thought for a second, and then replied, "no, Bianca, I am sorry but I cannot do that." Any spell that Bianca Rodrigues had held over him had been completely exorcised. He no longer wanted to have anything to do with her. He did not want to touch her, even if just to hold her hand. And her comfort was not his concern. The sirens grew louder, as if they were only a block or two away. Eric stood and stepped back, being careful to remain next to the car so that Bianca, if she were somehow able to summon the strength, could not run away.

He looked to his right, and saw Leticia walking to him in the rain. Moving in her direction, while still keeping his eyes on Bianca, he said, quietly, "it's over, *meu amor*, it's over." He broke down in tears, burying his head in Leticia's shoulder as she gently caressed his head with her hand. Leticia looked down into the car and saw Bianca Rodrigues sitting there, with her bruised face and split lip, and it took every fiber of her being not to leap into the front seat of the car and beat her beyond recognition.

"*Sua porca, você não merece ser mãe* (You pig, you don't deserve to be a mother)," she said as she looked down on Bianca. Bianca moved her head slightly to the right, sighed, and began to cry. The sirens were now at a deafening volume, and the sky was filled with red lights. Leticia pulled Eric's head from her shoulder, wiped the tears from his face, and gently kissed his cheek. "The police are here, Eric. We're almost done."

Two members of the São Paulo police force slowly approached Leticia and Eric. "*O que aconteceu aqui?* (What happened here?)" one of the officers asked. Leticia answered on Eric's behalf. She told the police about what had happened in Newark, about why Eric was there, and about the accident on the *Marginal Tiete*. She explained that the two girls in her car were Bianca's, and that they were both fine with the exception of a few cuts. Most importantly, she told the officer that Bianca was prepared to confess to the murder of her husband in the United States and clear Eric's name.

The officer called to his partner, who was speaking with Steve outside of the other car, "*você reconhece os nomes Eric Goldberg e Bianca Rodrigues?* (do you recognize the names Eric Goldberg and Bianca Rodrigues?)"

The other officer asked Steve to wait for a second, and walked over to the side of Jose Neto's car. "*Sim. Recebemos algo sobre eles hoje dos Estados Unidos. Por que?* (Yes, I do. We received something about them today from the United States. Why?)"

"Officer," Eric answered, "*meu nome e* Eric Goldberg. The woman in the car is Bianca Rodrigues. We are the people that you are supposed to look for. Ms. Rodrigues has something to tell you."

"*Senhora Rodrigues? Você tem algo a me dizer?* (Do you have something to tell me?)" asked the officer, leaning into the vehicle as he addressed Bianca Rodrigues.

"*Sim, eu tenho,*" she said softly, "yes, I do." She began to tell the story to the officers, with Leticia translating for Eric to make sure that her narrative was correct. She told the officers about her difficult life with Joao Rodrigues, about making plans with Jose to eliminate her husband, and about how she went to see Eric for a divorce even though she knew that she was going to try to kill him. She told the police that Jose, a mechanic, told her which wires or hoses she could cut so that Joao would lose control of the vehicle but it should look like an accident. She told the police how she had stolen the scissors from Eric's office and then planted them in the back of her husband's vehicle so that if there was any suspicion of foul play, it would lead to Eric and not her.

She also told the police that her letter to the Newark police was a complete lie, and that Eric had nothing at all to do with the accident, the murder, or her plans to murder her husband.

Leticia's eyes were welling with tears as she completed her translation, and Eric felt both the weight of the world being lifted off his shoulders and a feeling that he was going to pass out from nervousness. His knees buckled slightly, but Leticia again grabbed him and held him so that he would not fall. One of the officers turned to Eric and said, in English, "Mr. Goldberg, it sounds like you have been through a lot of trouble for no reason. I will call the police department in Newark and tell them what Ms. Rodrigues just told me, so you will be able to return home with no problems. I apologize on behalf of our country for her actions, and hope that the rest of your stay here, with this beautiful woman, is enjoyable."

"Thank you so much, officer, I really appreciate it," Eric replied. "Can you please speak to Detective Bailey when you call Newark?" He looked at Leticia. "We are not together, by the way."

"Don't correct him," Leticia interrupted, "thank you officer, for all that you have done for him," she blushed, "and thank you for calling me beautiful. I can't believe I look at all good in this rain."

"You do look beautiful," Eric said to her, "but why did you want him to think we are together?"

"Why shouldn't I?" she whispered. "He may think more of you if he thinks you have a young girlfriend. So play along, OK?" She turned back to the officer. "Officer," she called, "*Obrigada*. Thanks again for helping him. You have made us both very happy." She turned to Eric and kissed him on the lips, grabbing him in a strong embrace. His eyes opened in surprise, and he turned away from the police so that they would not see his shock at being kissed by Leticia. After a few seconds, he pulled away and started to walk to the car.

Leticia grabbed him, however, took his right hand, and placed it over her left breast. "Just so we are clear," she whispered, "her seios may be bigger than mine, but at least mine are real. Hers are *falsos*."

Eric knew what the word "*seios*" meant, having heard her use the term before and, especially in the context of her comment and the fact that his hand was currently resting on her breast. He decided that the time was finally right, however, for a little bit of levity. "What do you mean by '*seios*'," he asked, "is that some crazy Portuguese word for eyes? Because yes, she has large eyes, but I don't know how they could be fake."

"Not her *olhos*, *idiota*, her *seios*. Her, what's that word again, her boobs." She pushed his hand harder against her own breast so he could feel it moving under his touch. "See, this is what real feels like. Hers were fake." She removed his hand from her chest and her voice grew stern. "Never go with something fake, Eric. A person who tries to be fake in one way will, *naturalmente,* turn out to be *falso* in other ways. *Confia em mim.* Trust me."

Eric looked at his right hand, shook it, and then looked into her eyes.

"You are very bad, you know that?" he whispered to Leticia as they walked back to Steve's car. "And even with your little life lessons, it's a good thing that I don't take you seriously, or you may have gotten yourself into trouble back there."

"Nothing I can't handle," she said, smiling, as she walked over to Steve and took him in her arms. "It's over," she said to Steve. "She told the police everything."

Steve walked over to the officer who was standing by Jose's car, watching as the paramedics administered first aid to both Jose and Bianca. The other officer was in the squad car, on the phone. "Officer," he asked, "do you still need us here or can we leave? It's been a long morning, as you can imagine."

The officer looked at the squad car. "Stick around for just a minute or two." He motioned to his partner, who was on the phone. "He is on the phone with headquarters now, telling them what the woman just told him about what happened back in the States and down here. I think that Mr. Goldberg should stick around just in case he needs to fill in any details."

"Makes sense to me, officer," he replied. "Just let us know." He turned and walked back to his car, where Eric and Leticia were standing, and told them that the officer wanted for them to wait a little bit longer.

After five more minutes, the other officer emerged from his car and approached Eric. "Mr. Goldberg," he said, "again, my apologies for what you have been through. I called my captain and then typed everything out and sent it to him. He is on the phone now with the U.S. authorities, who will then contact your Detective Bailey. We will do everything we can to make sure that you are cleared of any problems. I don't know if you have a ticket to return home yet, but you will have no problems leaving our country or getting back into yours." He extended his hand. "We have your phone number, and Mr. Cooper here gave me his number. Here is my card, if you need anything from me. Good luck, sir. You may leave now."

Eric started to cry again as he shook the officer's hand, thanking him profusely. He turned and walked with Steve and Leticia back to their car. Before he sat down, however, he turned back toward the wreckage of the blue car. Leticia, standing next to him, did the same.

They watched as the paramedics placed a still unconscious Jose Neto on a backboard and gently lifted him into the ambulance. They watched as one of the officers playfully spoke to Carla and

Leila Rodrigues, letting them play with the siren on his car before having them sit in the backseat. As she sat, Carla waved to Leticia and mouthed *"obrigada"* to her, probably in thanks for helping her clean and bandage her cuts.

And they saw the other officer slowly pull a wincing Bianca Rodrigues out of Jose's car, place her in handcuffs, and help her into the ambulance with Jose. Leticia again hugged Eric as the ambulance drove away, and then they each opened their respective car doors, which had also been damaged in the impact, and sat down in silence.

"Uh, Steve," Eric called as the car door made a crunching sound as it opened, "I will pay for the damage to the car. Just let me know how much it is."

"I am sure that the insurance will take care of it," Steve replied as he opened the driver's side door, which was unscathed despite the two impacts. "So don't worry about it. If there is a deductible, then you will have to take me to a Yankees game the next time I visit my uncle."

"Make that both of us," Leticia chimed in. "Maybe I can learn a little something about baseball." She looked at Steve and smiled. "That way," she continued, "we can all talk about baseball and football, I mean soccer, right, Steve?"

Now Steve turned back to Eric and smiled. "That's true, *meu amor*," he replied.

"Besides," Leticia added, "that gives us a reason to come up during the winter. It's going to start getting colder here soon, so I think it may be time to plan a trip to New York in August."

"I would like that," Eric said as he carefully closed the creaking car door and fastened his seat belt.

CHAPTER XXVIII

Steve turned the car around and sped down the *Marginal Tiete* back toward home. "I guess we should go back to the apartment now and see if I can arrange a flight home so I get out of your hair," Eric said, "then you can have your lives back instead of taking care of me."

"Well, Eric, we've been thinking," said Steve, "why don't you stay here with us for a little while longer?"

"Yes," added Leticia from the back seat, "please stay with us. We can go out and enjoy ourselves now, rather than worrying about finding someone."

"And don't forget," Steve said, "the planetarium is open tomorrow. You know, the oldest one in the Southern Hemisphere," he looked back at Leticia and winked.

Eric's eyes again welled with tears. "Are you guys serious? I am going to cry again, even though I can't imagine that I have any more tears left in me."

"Please don't," pleaded Leticia. "If you cry then I am going to cry again. But we definitely want you to stay. Take a vacation. I think you deserve one."

"You're right," Eric said, "I could definitely use a vacation." He thought for a second. Can I make a couple of phone calls first?"

"Of course," Leticia answered, a broad smile growing across her face.

Eric pulled his cell phone out of his pocket, scrolled down his list of contacts, and pushed "call." After three rings, a nervous voice answered. "Hello, Eric, is that you?" the voice asked tentatively.

"Yes, honey, it is me. It all worked out. I will tell you when I get home, but she confessed to everything."

"That's amazing," Fatima shrieked. "I am so happy! Are you coming home now?"

"I don't think so," he said, looking into the back seat and grinning at Leticia. "If it is OK with you, I am going to stay here for a few more days. I think my schedule is clear for Monday anyway, and please just clear the rest of the week for me. I will let you know when I am coming back."

"That's fine with me, but what if someone gives me a hassle over adjourning something?"

"Just tell them tough shit, and that there are more important things in life. I have learned that, and they should also. And that I will deal with them when I get back." From the back seat, he could hear Leticia laughing. "I will talk to you soon," he said, and then added, "and Fatima, spend some time with your family this weekend and enjoy yourselves. I love you."

"I love and miss you, Eric," she replied. "Enjoy yourself and I will see you next week." Eric clicked off the phone, smiled, and looked over to Steve.

"So it sounds like you are staying," said Steve.

"How could I turn down such an invitation from you two? But I have to make one more call." Scrolling down a little more on his contacts list, he again pressed "call".

"Dad, is that you?" Jason's voice could be heard through the phone.

"Yes, it's me," Eric answered, cheerfully. "You spoke to Fatima, right?"

"She told me a pretty crazy story," Jason replied, "to be honest with you, I am a little pissed off that you didn't tell me any of this, but that can wait for now. I'm glad to hear from you. How did everything work out? I assume well since you sound happy."

"Let's just say that everything worked out just fine. I will give you the details when I see you. In fact, wait, hold on a minute," he said, cupping his hand over the phone. He turned back to Leticia and whispered, "would it be OK if I asked him to join me?"

"Of course," she said, "the more Goldbergs, the merrier."

"Jason," he said, bringing the phone back up to his face, "come down to São Paulo and spend a couple of days with your old man. It is beautiful down here."

"But ... I don't know if I can on such short notice," Jason said.

"Trust me, son," Eric told him, "there is never a good time to get away, and at the same time there is never a time that you cannot get away. Whatever is there will be waiting for you when you get back. When we get back to the apartment I will arrange for a flight for you, and will call you later with the information. You may have to fly from JFK, so why don't you look into a cab or car service now."

"OK, dad, if you insist, I would love to come down."

"That's the spirit, Jason," Eric said, his eyes again starting to moisten, "besides, I think it's a good time for us to start spending some quality father-son time together, just like we talked about before I left," he added, as a tear fell from his right eye. He could hear Leticia beginning to sniffle in the back seat.

"I couldn't agree more, dad," Jason responded. "I will start packing now, and will talk to you later."

Eric clicked off the phone, put it back in his pocket, and smiled as he looked out the window. As he did, the raindrops eased slightly. Rain continued to fall, but off in the distance, he could see beams of sunlight breaking through the haze. To Eric, it signaled not only the upcoming end of the rain, but also, in a greater sense, the beginning of his new life. A life where he would try to enjoy himself more, spend more time with his son, and, also, to be thankful for what he had and that he had come through this episode in his life without further damage.

"You know," Leticia said as she placed her hand on Eric's shoulder, "I have a younger sister. She's 18 now. And if you think I am pretty, you should see her. How old is Jason?"

"Be careful with this one, Eric," warned Steve, "you don't want Jason to make the same mistake I made."

Eric turned to his left and kissed Leticia's hand. "You know what," he said, "he could do much worse. And you certainly could have done much worse than this beautiful angel." Leticia leapt forward, reached her head around the back of the seat, and kissed Eric on the left cheek. "Besides," Eric continued, "I can certainly get used to coming down here a couple of times a year to visit. Now where can you go to get a good breakfast in this city? I am starving."

"I know a place," Leticia said, "Steve, keep driving. I will tell you where to turn. And Eric," she said, "I should warn you. My sister is really wild. She makes me look, how would you say, conservative."

"Is that even possible?" asked Eric, as both Leticia and Steve began to laugh. "If that is true, then once we set up Jason's flight, we should give her a call to come and meet him." He turned to Leticia. "If there is anything I have learned on this trip, *meu amor,* not to sound too preachy, is that you have to live a little, and try not to regret the choices that you have made along the way. The boy may as well learn it now, before it is too late."

"It's never too late, though," Leticia responded. "You just learned it, and you are pretty darned old, you *velho.* Then again, it may be too late for Bianca, right?"

Eric smiled. "Yes it is," he answered, "but she will learn that being trapped in a bad situation does not justify what she did." He looked out the window, as the rays of sunlight seemed to be increasing in number. "Maybe one day, she will be able to enjoy herself again. At least that would be good for her kids' sake."

"You know, Eric," Leticia said, "you're pretty cute when you smile. Steve, *meu amor,*" she added, turning to Steve, "maybe it is time for you to share me with someone else, someone who is older than you."

Steve gasped in horror. "Sure, I guess that would be OK, he said, sarcastically, "and then," he paused, thinking, "think about it. If you guys got married and Jason and your sister got married, you would be her sister and mother-in-law. And Eric would be your husband and your daughter's father-in-law." He smiled. "Some would say that this could happen in the redneck areas of the states, but I disagree. Clearly it could only happen in Brazil."

"Yes," Eric said, laughing and repeating Steve's comment in his best attempt at a Portuguese accent. *"so no Brasil.* Only in Brazil. Thank God. *Graças a Deus."*

Leticia looked back at Eric and laughed. She then turned back around and looked out of the car's front windshield as the rain continued to slow and sunlight started to illuminate the city of São Paulo. Her face burst into a wide smile, content with the knowledge that she had accomplished both of her goals that morning. She had witnessed the sight of Bianca Rodrigues being placed into handcuffs. And, as the familiar chorus of Gilberto Gil's version of *"Three Little Birds"* echoed through her mind, she also took pleasure in seeing Eric Goldberg smiling and laughing, seemingly truly happy for what she believed to be the first time in months. Just like she had promised Eric, everything for him was, in fact, now alright.

THE END

Made in the USA
Charleston, SC
10 February 2013